Did Father Michael, Who Came to America, Find Success?

Did Father Michael, Who Came to America, Find Success?

Rev. Thaddeus M. Swirski, Ph.D.

James C. Winston
Publishing Company, Inc.
Trade Division of Winston-Derek Publishers Group, Inc.

TO SOW THE FALLOW SOIL

© 1997 by James C. Winston Publishing Company, Inc.

First printing

Top illustration on page ii, symbol of the Roman Catholic Diocese of Cleveland, used by permission of Father Ralph Wiatrowski, Chancellor.
Bottom right illustration on page ii, symbol of the Army Chaplaincy, used by permission of the Pentagon Office of the Chief Chaplaincy of the United States Army.
Bottom left illustration, symbol of the University of Richton, used by permission of the artist, Amanda Shumway-Tate.

Cover illustration by Amanda Shumway-Tate.

PUBLISHED BY JAMES C. WINSTON PUBLISHING COMPANY, INC.
Trade Division of Winston-Derek Publishers Group, Inc.
Nashville, Tennessee 37205

Library of Congress Catalog Card No: 95-62186
ISBN: 1-55523-780-0

Printed in the United States of America

To The Most Reverend A. James Quinn,
Auxiliary Bishop of Cleveland,
whose advice and encouragement supported the author
in bringing this book to completion,
and also inspired him and other priests with his kindness
by his example as a brotherly priest
in the commitment in the pastoral ministry.

The writer is also grateful to his friends who also helped
and encouraged him to write this book.

To: MY DEAR FRIEND AND PARISHIONER
LT. CASIMER WHO SHARES WITH ME
COMMON MEMORY WITH FRIENDSHIP
FROM THE FIRST POLISH ARMY DURING
WORLD WAR II.
WITH BEST WISHES FOR YOU
AND FOR YOUR FAMILY.

Rev. S. Leinski

COL. CHAPLAIN

Contents

Forward

Readers who know Father Michael as *The Priest Who Came to America* will enjoy this sequel which tells more about his struggles as foreigner, newcomer and priest in the small urban parish of St. Agatha's. Looking back on the occasion of his twentieth anniversary at St. Agatha's and his forty years as a priest, Father Michael "counts his graces", first and foremost of which is the spiritual well-being of his parishioners and the material well-being of his parish. The book is filled with touching, often humorous anecdotes showing how Father Michael met many obstacles and received much help over the years and came to love St. Agatha's and find increasing satisfaction in his vocation.

But Father Michael wishes to do more than entertain the reader. In describing his closeness to his parishioners, his pleasure in performing his priestly duties, his delight in caring for the lawn and flowers, he hopes to encourage others to enter the life he has chosen and loves.

The book shows that, although the parish is small, Father Michael's ministry has always been one of reaching out beyond its boundaries. He touches the lives of students, faculty and administrators of the University of Richton; of officers and cadets in the United States Army; of Polish diplomats; of Richton city officials and many others. And now through this book he wishes to reach all Americans.

Father Michael is very concerned about the crime, vandalism and fear which he experiences daily in the streets near the parish and describes in many incidents in the book. He calls on America, his beloved adopted country, to save itself by returning to reverence, love and respect for family, Church and God.

Marjorie Greenberger
Professor Emeritus
The University of Akron
English Department

Preface

The following pages will recount the experiences of Father Michael Panski who was introduced to readers in my first book, *The Priest Who Came to America*.

In that book I told the story of his life in Poland during World War II, focusing on his life in an orphanage, his trials and tribulations during the German occupation, his military service, his seminary preparation for the priesthood, and his ordination. Father Michael's subsequent emigration to America and the early years of priestly service were also delineated.

In this second volume, I will concentrate on his life as a pastor of a small, predominantly Polish parish in Richton, Ohio. The accelerated changes in American society and the Catholic Church, as well as the social and moral issues of the day, presented formidable challenges which Father Michael attempted to meet. How he met these challenges is revealed through the personal and ministerial experiences of his priestly journey.

This novel is based on true stories. All names, places, churches and institutions are fictional to protect their privacy and, in some instances, their safety.

Reverend Thaddeus M. Swirski, Ph.D.

1

Difficulties and Achievements

In one's life it is impossible for everything to go smoothly. So it is in Father Michael's life. But he very strongly believes that the difficulties help him to achieve the great goals in his life, by making him stronger, not by complaining, but by working hard. Of course, achievement is the result not only of his personal involvement to his commitment, but also thanks to God and his friends. So, in this book, and partially in this chapter, there are many descriptions of pleasant and unpleasant situations that Father Michael goes through.

As I sit here under the newly painted gazebo and look at the statue of St. Jude, I start to reexamine the nearly forty years of priesthood. I look at both the good and the not so good that has occurred in those years.

At first it is the worst that enters my mind. Even before I came to America I found that even some of the clergy can be different. Shortly after my ordination while I was still in my native Poland, I encountered Monsignor Maxim Otto. He was one who liked to play cards and enjoyed his drinks and his social activities. Monsignor Otto, dressed in the purple of his office and decorated with a huge gold cross, asked if I like to play cards and to drink.

I answered, "I neither drink nor play cards."

"So, what do you do for recreation and relaxation?" the older gray-haired priest asked.

"I study theology and enjoy military science," I replied.

"Well, keep your rifle. Someday they may need you, but you will not be able to associate with the rest of the world if you do not play cards nor drink some highballs. And don't try to tell us what you learned in the seminary; that is something we know, too," said the monsignor.

It was then that I went outside where the children were playing, and I enjoyed watching them as they romped around. They looked at me descending the steps of the cathedral and ran excitedly towards me with their smiling faces. This was more enjoyable than playing cards. This reminded me that Jesus had said that, to enter the Kingdom of Heaven, we have to become like little children.

It was then, at twenty-four, that I realized that I was closer to the children than to the older people. I was happy about that, and I knew then that I was a long way from learning how to drink and to play cards or to be at the level of socializing with monsignors.

Several Sundays later I stopped at the same cathedral for mass. Father Maxim asked me to preach the High Mass where many priests, as well as other faithful people, were present. I walked nervously to the high pulpit which reached halfway to the ceiling, and I felt dizzy from the height. I hesitated briefly, crossed myself, and began my sermon. I don't remember what the subject was, but I felt happy later because many people complimented me on the sermon.

I also remember my first assignment in the small town of Dobre Miasto. What few possessions I had were in a box tied with a rope. There were books, prayer books, and a Bible which I had inherited from a monsignor who had been executed by the Secret Police of the Polish Communist Party. Two of the other books in the collection were *Anna Karenina* and *War and Peace*. These I had inherited from a retired Russian professor whom I had met not too far from Moscow while I was serving in the First Division of the Polish army. Professor Jan Pavlov gently handed me the yellowed books and told me to read them. He also said that perhaps one day I might teach great Russian literature. How could he possibly have known?

So began my journey to Dobre Miasto, which is Polish for *Good City*. I smiled at the people who too were going the same way, but they just looked at me without changing expressions. They called me Brother, not Father. I guess that I looked too young to be a priest. The trip was very unpleasant; the road was bumpy, and I had to stand leaning against a seat where two plump women were gossiping. Finally, the bus driver announced our arrival and that we must get off the bus.

Many buildings had been destroyed, and the sidewalks were full of debris. I walked slowly through the city until I saw the church tower. I approached the rectory and rang the bell to the side door. I heard a deep voice within call out, "Marianna, answer the door."

"It looks like your assistant has arrived," Marianna answered. "He looks so very young!"

She opened the door and asked me my name. They were expecting me, and so began my new life.

I submerged myself in my duties as an assistant pastor. Some of the most pleasant experiences included telling stories to the children of the town. Other rewards were getting to know the older people of the town. However, many of the older parishioners felt that I was not old enough to understand their pain and suffering. I didn't want them to know that I, too, was wise to pain and suffering, so I never told them of my years in the orphanage, being in the army, and in the underground.

After some time I became ill and began to grow weak. I often wished that God would take me to Heaven. My health was not good, and my life was not happy. I had no one but God and the Virgin Mary to care about me. But I also realized that Divine Providence had need of me.

The authorities in the city wanted the teenagers to come to the city hall for lectures on contraception. Since these young people were innocent, I encouraged them to come to church and pray to the Virgin Mary for help and not to go to the city hall for those lectures. For doing this I was arrested as an enemy of modern education in the Polish People's Republic.

Even this was part of God's Providence. While I was in jail, God used me to help the daughter of a Polish prison officer prepare for her First Communion. In the month of my incarceration, I prepared her and said a private mass and gave her her First Communion.

But living in such a difficult place continuously made me long to come to the United States. Finally, my dream came true and I came to America.

Even here there were weeks and months of adjustments. Here, too, I was an assistant pastor and was on probation. I thought that I could be used successfully in a Polish-American parish, but it was not easy at that time because there was a lot of prejudice against foreign-born priests in this country.

Finally, however, I got the chance to be a pastor in a Polish-American parish. I was very excited and looked forward to being able to serve God and the people who needed me.

As I continue to recall the past years, I thank God that I am now in the United States of America. It has been forty years since my ordination, and what I had hoped for in my life has mostly come true. I realize that Divine Providence has provided for me over these years.

What a beautiful summer day when I arrived at St. Agatha's Church. It was noon on July 17, 1974—the traditional hour for the beginning of one's pastoral assignment. I was as fearful as I was happy.

It was such a strange day. I was not greeted by any of the parishioners, nor by the former pastor, who told me that he was in a hurry to leave and that he did not have time for me. It seems that he was on the way to the bank. Later I discovered that he had withdrawn a significant amount of the parish operational funds and set up a scholarship fund which could not be touched for the use of the parish.

I certainly did not feel welcome. The rectory door was locked, and I had no key. The pastor had given the key to a nun who lived in the nearby convent, but she was very hostile. Also, she did not want to give me the key to the Tabernaculum, even when I asked for it. I carried a consecrated Host from the bishop as a sign of unity between the hierarchy and the parish, and I needed the key to place the Host there.

Soon the former pastor returned, but he was still not very friendly. He showed me the last cup of milk in the place, but told me that I could not drink it as it belonged to him.

After the former pastor departed, I went to the church to pray, and then back to the rectory to unpack my belongings. In spite of this difficult beginning, I felt strong because God was with me.

I soon discovered that I had no housekeeper, no janitor, and no assistant. I was all alone. I certainly was not the best cook, so I had little more than cold cuts and bread to eat. It took me eight months before I could find even a part-time housekeeper to come in twice a week.

One day as I sat on the floor of the dining room with tears in my eyes, I thanked God for giving me the opportunity to work and to fulfill my commitment, and I prayed that I would be challenged as a priest.

The beginning was not easy. I was not welcomed by either the nuns nor by my parishioners. On one of my first calls I got the suggestion that I take up a second collection to buy a one-way ticket to the country from which I had come.

Before and after Sunday Mass, the people were not friendly. There had been no announcement of my arrival in the Sunday bulletin. I later discovered that this priest had told the people of the parish that the foreign priest they were getting would not work hard and would eventually relinquish the parish to strange people. He told them to write to the bishop and ask that I be removed.

But something strange happened. The previous priest returned to get something he had forgotten. He smiled and told me to be careful, that the people were not nice, and that I should be glad that he was not staying at the rectory because he, himself, was a difficult man.

So it was that I began my pastorate. But as time passed there were people who began to speak to me and to bring me stuffed cabbages and other food. The altar boys became friendly and even came to mass on time. Things got better. I began to feel that I could someday melt the cold hearts of those who were in the parish.

I knew that working here would not be easy, but I was determined to stay. Perhaps the most difficult was the rejection. However, I was reminded of Christ's rejection; His own people had turned their backs on Him. Of course, there is no comparison between a humble servant like me and our Lord, but is not our Lord an example of the priestly vocation?

I always try to follow the teachings of Jesus. First of all, I try to forgive and to forget. As I think of this time, I smile. Who would have imagined that I would remain here for twenty years?

The people have changed. Some even tell me openly that they have learned to love me. I look at many whom I have baptized with fatherly affection. I performed marriages and prepared candidates for First Holy Communions and confirmations. These are my privileges. I also remember with sadness the funerals of some of the people whom I have loved.

Spiritually and materially, St. Agatha's parish is doing very well now.

Even though the parish is doing well, I realize that the shortage of priests is a serious problem and that many parishes are without spiritual leadership. Like many other priests, I am concerned about the future of the Church. I sometimes feel that the world is becoming more materialistic than at any other time in the history of mankind.

I often discuss these problems with my friend and student of mine at the university, David Long. He is young, but has already been in the service of his country. This time in the service has given him a maturity that others his age may not have.

"What will happen to our churches and synagogues?" he once asked.

"Certainly, if we don't have churches, we will need more jails. We will always need someone to encourage us when we get depressed and are suffering. We must realize that there is more than material good; there is God, a supernatural being who loves us. His son was sent to save us, not to condemn us," I told him.

"He calls young men to proclaim His Gospel, who sacrifice their lives for God's glory and the benefit of human beings. All the problems that society knows now—violence, drug abuse, rape, and thievery—will increase if more people stop believing in God and His Commandments and in the right of people to live peacefully in society."

As we continued our discussion, I commented that David would be a pleasant person to have as an assistant, but he said that he would never want to be celibate.

"I consider married life to be very important, and a very big commitment. Families are very important, so when you marry, be a good husband and father," I said.

David continued, "I don't know whether I can afford to marry. Do you realize how expensive it is to raise children now?"

"We don't count married life based on materialistic things," I said, "but on love and understanding. These things should be our goals."

"But I hear many young people talk about not wanting children or any commitments," said David.

I replied, "One day they will realize that it is natural to follow God's precept to perpetuate a new generation. We are responsible to the generations yet to come. Ministers of the Church have much to do to encourage this generation not to be so selfish, but to share their spiritual and material wealth with their children and those generations to come.

"It is surprising how large families sometimes survive better than small families and live with the blessings of God. They are often successful, very well educated, and accepted by society because they know how to respect others and to live peaceful lives."

David looked at me and asked, "Aren't you ever lonely? I often think that you must be because you spend so many long evenings alone."

I tried to tell him that a person like me is not lonely because I am always busy. I have my priestly obligations, and the administration of the parish, and my teaching. I also told him of the grass cutting in the summer, and the shoveling of snow in the winter, and keeping the church and rectory in good repair.

"By the way," David said, "your pay is very low."

"I have a car and enough to eat," I replied. "We have hospitalization that we did not have years ago, and we also have retirement benefits. Above all, we have the satisfaction of being what we are. Do you know what it means to help someone when he needs you or to comfort someone who is depressed or is going to jail for the rest of his life?

"And what about saying mass every day in commemoration of the greatest man who ever lived? It is an honor to be His servant.

"I know that by the year 2000 there will be a serious shortage of priests," I continued, "but instead of counting on figures spewed from computers, we should be praying to God that He will send young people to work in His vineyard, whether in the priesthood or in some other area of religious life.

"Jesus once said that whatever we ask for will be given through faith in His Father. My faith is strong that the Church will not be allowed to disappear."

David said that he understood and that he hoped that I was right.

Some priests of the Roman Catholic Church are very gifted; some not only have beautiful voices, but use their voices to artistically perform their liturgical services. Others are good counselors, speakers, chaplains in hospitals, teachers in religious schools. A few are equipped and prepared for teaching and lecturing on a university level. Even the armed forces attract some of them. Some of the young, especially assistant priests, give time to coach sports in Catholic schools.

Besides having in my heart a call to the pastoral ministry, I, too, use some of my training in a second profession. I enjoy teaching at the university level in the Modern Languages Department at the

University of Richton. I am so happy that the Church authorities allow me to do so because I consider the university my second home. Since the age of eighteen as a student at the seminary, I have taught. Gradually, I have gone from teaching at elementary schools to teaching college.

I really have two groups of students—my C.C.D. classes and my classes at the University of Richton.

The students who come for religious instructions are cordial and friendly. They are anxious to learn about Jesus and his Church. I always want to teach them gently about Catholic doctrines, knowledge about God, the human destiny. After this earthly life, I point out, there is an eternal life prepared for us by God who loves us.

Sometimes these groups are small, sometimes large; it depends on how the parents respond.

I believe it is a privilege to instruct C.C.D. classes for the parish.

After one of the classes, one of the parents stopped me because he wanted to talk. He said, "Father, I do like to be in the classroom when you teach the basics of our faith, as it is good to review what I studied a long time ago as a child."

I was very pleased to hear this and told him that he was always welcome in the classes.

Soon afterwards the father mentioned watching one of the *Sixty Minutes* programs where it seemed to him that the Church was being attacked by the news media. The program talked about the Church losing many faithful people. The program also discussed the fact that ex-nuns were attacking the Church and questioning the pope's authority. This was very disturbing to this parent.

"Yes," I replied, "it is sad, but didn't Jesus say that to follow in His footsteps would not be easy?

"But, too bad," I continued, "they don't mention that, during the time of this present saintly Pope John Paul II, the Catholic Church is reaching almost a billion of the faithful.

"History shows that from time to time the Church suffers persecution, accusations, and harassment; should we be different now and not have the privilege to suffer for God and a good cause?

"If we have departures of some priests from the priesthood or faithful people from the Church, it is not the problem and fault of the Church; it is a problem of society."

As we continued our discussion, I said, "We are a spoiled society; we have everything, and we are not hungry as people in other places. We just do not respect any authority. So, if we are bad, that is the kind that will create a future society and part of it will be the clergy. But, I do believe strongly that, as a priest serving my church, the Holy Spirit will protect and defend our faith."

The university group is very different. First, they are adults, and most of them are serious about their studies; they work hard mentally and physically and often work at part-time jobs to help pay the tuition. Some of these students have problems and are upset by the friendly atmosphere in the classroom. Maybe Johnnie's girlfriend broke up with him last night, or he has a hangover and cannot enjoy the environment of the classroom. I realize that the students often do not have someone to talk with about their problems, so I try to listen and to counsel them as best as I can.

It is good to be with young people and to be in touch with knowledge. Religion and knowledge have so much in common that I have no problems with connecting theology, philosophy and literature; it also helps in my pastoral ministry.

Learning a language is not always an easy matter. It requires repetition and memorization, as well as organizational skills. My specialization is in Slavic studies. The fulfillment of my life's desire and dream has been realized through teaching at the university.

The first semester of classes is always a little uneasy as the students and instructor size each other up. I try to begin the class by introducing myself and shaking hands with each of the students. I also encourage them to study and to do their homework from the first day.

Semesters usually proceed smoothly for the class. I have taught for sixteen years and there has never been a serious problem in the classroom. Some students need more encouragement to make the best of their time and to finish their studies, and I am always willing to give them this encouragement.

I guess one could say that I am a conscientious and demanding instructor who means business and doesn't want to waste time. I want the students to benefit from the class. I also consider myself a friend of the students, as well as their teacher, and they respond kindly to me. Sometimes students approach me privately to discuss a problem with their studies or in their personal lives. I understand them because I remember the difficult circumstances I encountered in Poland and in the U.S.A. graduate school in their country because, along with my studies, I had many other obligations as a priest and a teacher. The educational system which I went through was challenging for me and prepared me for teaching Slavic subjects, especially Russian and Polish languages and literature. I like to see my students make progress in the mastery of the language. In the classroom the students learn to sing in Russian and to recite poems, which help them to improve the pronunciation of these difficult languages.

I can remember feeling somewhat reluctant to become too involved with other faculty members. After all, I was a foreigner, and also a priest, not like the other academicians. I remember also when I met Dr. Robert Currey, then the president of the University of Richton. Sister Anne sent me an invitation for a reception of the new president of the university.

When I arrived, she said, "I want you to come to meet the new president of the University of Richton. He has visited many other places and has accepted our invitation here to the Newman Center.

"But," she continued, "Father Kenny Smithe left the priesthood and now we need a priest here at the center and I was hoping that you would like to take over those duties."

So there was more to the invitation than I at first thought. It turned out to be a very pleasant gathering. President Currey and his wife welcomed me and I felt that this gentle and well-educated man was sent by God to this position at the university.

We soon became friends. When the Slavic Society, of which I am the faculty adviser, sponsored activities, the president always tried to attend and to encourage me to continue to help the students.

Not only did President Currey support university activities, he also came to the 75th anniversary of St. Agatha's Church and participated in the mass and spoke at the banquet which followed. But the most touching moment was when he spoke of his visit to Eastern Europe and his mention of his visit to Warsaw, the capital of Poland.

"When I was in Warsaw," he said, "I thought about you, Michael. Life sent you so many miles away from your fatherland."

"I am so happy that you mentioned your visit. It makes me feel so good to know that you have visited my homeland," I said.

I soon realized that changes are not easy for people in charge of institutions such as presidents and directors, but changes are also difficult and challenging for people who work under them. When people whom one becomes close to have to leave, we miss them. That is how I feel about those friends, such as Robert Currey, who is now president of another large university, and others with whom I had long associations who are also gone. They were kind, compassionate, and understanding and supported and encouraged me and others who worked with them. I still pray for them and remember our friendly lunches.

I see what success I have had reflected through the response of parishioners to me and in their attendance at services and parish functions. Though I do not organize polka masses and sausage dinners after services, I still see the serious involvement of the people when they prepare themselves for the sacraments and when they talk with me. They are my people, and I feel close to them.

I know that good friends help a priest do his best and help him have a feeling of satisfaction that his commitment is working. It is evident when some call and ask me how I am.

Everything can be done for God's glory with the help and encouragement of friends. There are many of them in the parish of St. Agatha.

Friends are everywhere, not just in the parish. One evening before Palm Sunday, Father Bob Betner came to St. Agatha's to visit me and to help with Holy Week ceremonies. Father Bob is French Canadian and a candidate for a doctorate in theology. He is a gentleman who brought a great deal of companionship to me. We met at St. Patrick's Church in Ottawa, Canada, when I was studying for my doctorate.

But this was to be his last visit. He told me that he was going on a sabbatical from his priestly duties. His bishop, a gentleman from Prince George Island, had granted him this time off to rest.

This was not just a sabbatical; it was the first step in his departure from the service of Christ and toward married life. I was surprised because I believed that he would return to the ministry.

When the Holy Week ceremonies were over, we discussed the positive and negative aspects of the priesthood. We both agreed that it is a privilege to be called to the service of God and the people of God, but the pastoral ministry is not easy.

Bob said, "Michael, I still remember when I was ordained." There were tears in his eyes.

"There was no doubt that there was no greater calling in one's life than to work for God," he continued.

"What do you know about parish work?" I asked him. "You have always worked for the bishop and taught in high school."

I asked him, "Do you want to know what parish life is like? If you are in a small parish, you are not only the pastor, but the housekeeper and the janitor as well.

"Bob, did you like what we had for breakfast? It wasn't like that when I started here. It was funny. When I first came here, I went to church and left eggs cooking on the stove. When I returned, they had exploded all over the kitchen. And the time I burned the potatoes and hamburger, the rectory was filled with the smoke, and I could smell the burning items in the church when I said mass. As soon as I finished with mass, I ran to the rectory. The smell lingered for two days. That is one of my experiences as I was learning to cook.

"And what if you are giving a sermon and you start to wonder if you turned off the stove so the pork chops would not burn or if you turned off the iron? It happens when you do everything around the rectory."

Bob looked at me and said, "Keep up the good work. They didn't tell us at the seminary what we would have to do, did they?"

Then he asked me to tell him more about my experiences as a pastor, about my everyday life.

I continued, "You have to be disciplined to get up on time. Remember when you were scheduled last year to help say mass? When you overslept, I got up and went to the church without even shaving. But, I didn't complain because I know that, when we study, we really get tired. I can't afford to oversleep. It is my obligation to provide mass."

"Will you forgive me, Michael?" asked Bob.

"Getting up is not the most difficult thing to do. I enjoy getting up to say mass. I think how nice it is to be able to commemorate every day the Last Supper of our Lord.

"After mass, on the way to the rectory, I notice the lovely flowers. They make me feel happy. I often think how great is God's splendor. If God cares about a small flower, then He must certainly care about the people He created in His image.

"When the first obligation of the day is completed, I go to the university to teach. It helps me keep a balance in my life. Contact with youths keeps me young, at least in my mind.

"Bob, despite what people say about young people, I know they are able and that they work hard, especially at the university. They have goals. Many are pleasant, and I have made friends with some of them. Usually, when the semester is over, I am a little sad that they will not be in my classes anymore," I said.

"Michael, you are doing well when you can do two things at the same time. We have something in common. I have the same feelings, but I don't want to cook for myself and I would never accept a small parish. Also, I am no good at taking care of flowers," replied Bob.

As I listened to Bob, I thought how good it is to have the yard filled with flowers and lovely trees that my friend Joe Hernik and I planted. The trees are like friends. They shade the rectory and make the air easier to breathe.

Bob asked, "Aren't your evenings lonely?"

"No," I said. "I have office hours in the evening and also instructions. Sometimes young couples who are unsure about the future come to speak to me as they prepare for marriage. They love each other and want to be married in the Church. They often have questions and hopes, and I try to help them.

"Sometimes giving instructions brings us closer to God. And I like to say only the best about our faith. The teachings of our Lord are so simple, more so than we have made them. Remember when a lawyer asked the Lord what he had to do to enter the Kingdom of Heaven and Christ responded, 'You are right when you say love God and love your neighbor as yourself;' it is the foundation of all precepts."

I noticed a spark in Bob's eyes as he said, "I agree with you; our Lord is great."

"You cannot be lonely if you are committed," I continued. "After office hours and instruction, I watch the news and correct papers and prepare for my classes. Of course, I continue to say the priestly Breviary. The readings and prayers are directed to our Archpriest who protects and strengthens us throughout our priestly lives. My soul rests when I am alone. No one disturbs me. Since I have been with people all my life, including growing up with four hundred other children, then going into the army and on to the seminary, I am happy to be alone now. But I do enjoy having your company now and your help with weekend services.

"Now it is time that we both get some sleep. Remember, you have to get up to help with mass in the morning."

St. Agatha's parish is not only my concern, but that of the parish council as well. These people give advice and support and help to back up my commitment.

I never expected to have male and female Eucharistic ministers, but I have learned to respect their faithful assistance, and commentators add splendor through their beautiful readings.

There are a few difficulties in pastoral ministry, but most of the time I really enjoy my involvement in the spiritual life of the parish.

I like to give instructions for the sacraments and review of the doctrines of the Church for parents of children who are to be baptized. There is also joy in giving First Communion instructions and for Confirmation. I like to share the knowledge of the Church with my parishioners, as well as the joy of great celebrations such as weddings, but also the pain and sadness of a funeral.

My most beautiful moments are to celebrate the Holy Liturgy. Even though the parish is not large, I love to see people with their beautiful and friendly faces. It is wonderful to listen to them sing both in English and in Polish.

I realize that to be a mediator between people and God is my greatest privilege, and it gives me great joy. I understand that, because of this honor of my ordination, I am able to serve God's people and that they need me.

I know most of my parishioners by their first names and most of their relatives as well. Sometimes I see new people come to church; occasionally, I see one of my students, even though they may not be Catholic.

Sermons provide the opportunity for communicating God's love to the people. There are many positive aspects of the Catholic faith. We are not created by God for dying, but for living forever and for God's glory and for our benefit. I stress that we must examine ourselves from time to time and reconcile with God. Reconciliation allows us to attain eternal life.

I also stress that the world is often a difficult place. Sometimes evil seems to prevail, but the positive aspect is that God is with us. And if God is with us, who can be against us?

Occasionally, I just slam the door to forget about my obligations and turn on the answering machine in case there is an important message or an emergency call. Though I have developed a sense of self-discipline, I realize that there are times in my life when I am weak, but still I must continue to fulfill my obligations.

A thing that greatly bothers me is the way children behave. They are so beautiful when they are little. As they get older, they become so noisy as they sit in church with their parents. Mostly I enjoy seeing the little ones with their parents, but when they misbehave, it is disturbing, especially outside the church.

Though there have been many good moments in my life here at St. Agatha's, there is an incident that has disturbed me for a long time.

Many days when I walk to the church I enjoy the trees and flowers. They remind me of God's greatness. I remember one spring day as I went to the church. Before I went in, I saw a bird that was hurt in the front of a tree. Since there was no time before mass, I couldn't take care of it. It was quiet, but I heard children walking and swearing as they made their way to school. It was nothing new, though; they always acted like that.

Once inside the church, I tried to concentrate on my meditations but heard wild screaming and knocking outside. They were throwing gravel.

After mass I left the church to look for the bird. It was in the parking lot, dead and covered with stones. I realized what had happened. The bird was smashed, and the children were gone. I picked up the stones and carried the bird away.

I tried to bury it in the ground with dignity. This incident really upset me. If they killed a helpless bird, I felt certain that they had no faith in God, nor respect for living things. Some of them were certain to grow up to be corrupt.

Overhead, adult birds flew by, singing their melody of sorrow, grieving for their baby. Human beings did not help it to survive, but cut short its life. They killed with malice of forethought and cruelty.

"Awake, America, awake," I lamented. "Nature and God—if you do not love them, you are worse than wild animals who at least only kill to survive."

As a war veteran and a faculty member at the university, as a writer and a pastor, I wish to help and to protect and to defend, but not to torture the innocent or wounded.

I called the principal of the high school. I offered my time to talk to the children—I knew they were in trouble. The principal promised me that he would invite me to talk to the teenagers, but the call never came.

Some children who are not with their parents often use language that reflects a lack of family guidance. They talk loudly and scream.

They do not seem interested in going to school; they are often late and fight as they go and disturb other people in the neighborhood.

They have very little respect for people's property. Once as I came home, the yard looked like an oriental blanket with my flowers where the children had pulled them out and had thrown them on the ground around the rectory.

The next day when I saw them, I asked them why they had destroyed the flowers; they just smiled at me. They seemed to think it was cute. I will never understand their behavior.

The statue of the Virgin Mary, which stands in front of the church, was defaced by some children using an iron pipe. Her child's hand was destroyed and her face beat up. I tried to understand that some children are not brought up to respect religious things, but can no one teach them to respect places that are holy to other people? We are blessed with freedom of religion, but we do not like to be disturbed by people who do not care.

I remember reading in the local newspaper about a bishop in Virginia. He was a very devoted man who, after several years as a bishop, took early retirement. He announced that the reason for his retirement was that parents do not care about their children's spiritual life. If they do not go to church, the parents are responsible. Even more disturbing is that the younger generation does not show love for God or for vocations such as the priesthood or other religious careers.

"The bishop is right," I thought. "Some people do not blame the parents. They frequently tell me that their children cannot come to church because they need their sleep because of jobs they have, even though we have three masses on Sunday and one on Saturday. These parents should tell their children that forty minutes or more once a week to praise God and thank Him for health and graces is not too much to ask.

"Pity the poor human heart if it is linked only to material things."

Later I went to the church to pray. *I hope that future generations will begin to see the value in having faith and belief in a compassionate and loving God. He provides us with Fatherly care and will welcome us into Heaven.*

I remember when I first came to St. Agatha's; I called Anthony Ball, the bishop's secretary, to tell him of some of my concerns.

"I see that there are unkind people everywhere," said Father Ball. "But remember that the Son of God also suffered when people rejected Him, mocked Him, and crucified Him. Who are you to complain? Just think about Christ."

So now when I become upset about people, I remember what Father Ball said.

I know that in the ministry it is important to be in good health. After I had been at St. Agatha's for many years, I decided to see a doctor. I was very shocked to discover that I had developed ulcers. I promised that I would cooperate with the doctor and follow his advice. He recommended that I do things that I like to do to ease the stress, something more pleasant than listening to the problems of the people.

One of the doctor's suggestions was that I should get plenty of rest. I smiled when the doctor said this. I wondered how, with all my duties, I would be able to fulfill the doctor's orders.

But about that time spring break from the university came; it was indeed welcomed. I looked forward to rest and relaxation. However, with the appearance of spring comes yard work and other chores around the rectory and church. There was not much time to rest, so life went on.

But, as always, something good happens. For a long time, I had wanted to put a cross on the front of the church. Inside the church is beautiful with marble floors and walls. There are Italian paintings to help make the church feel like a place of worship. But on the outside the church/school building looks more like a place of business than a church, so the parish council and I decided to install a large wrought iron cross on the church building. It helps designate the building as a place to worship God. The cross was dedicated on Good Friday.

The day after the dedication of the cross, as I went to get office supplies, I discovered that a window in the church was broken. As I arrived at the office supply store, I saw that the door was open so

I went in. I met the president of the company, and he said that for me whatever I bought that day would be 50% off.

How could I be upset about the broken window when someone else had been so generous? I considered myself lucky.

I also found that the chalices from which I distribute Holy Communion had begun to show wear from the many years of use. When I discovered how much it would cost to repair them, I was very surprised at how expensive it was. But, I put the chalices in a bag and prayed that I could find a more reasonable place to have the work done.

I remembered two brothers who had graduated from the same university where I teach. They own a company that does body work on cars, and I wondered if they could use the same process on the chalices as they used on cars.

I decided to stop to talk with them. I put the chalices on the table and asked them if what I wanted was possible for them. Wes and Scott North looked at the chalices. I really expected a negative reply, but to my surprise, they said they could do the job. I offered to pay for their work, but they refused.

A few days later they informed me that the work was finished. I sent them a letter of thanks and two bottles of wine for their Easter dinner.

The three buildings at St. Agatha's need to be checked each spring for repairs. One is the care and maintenance of the roofs. Each year I must check for cracks and leaks, and if repairs are needed, I must find at least three contractors to come to give estimates for the cost. If the cost is over the amount permitted by the diocese, I must contact their office for the final decision concerning who will do the work.

Other expenses include boilers. They are often difficult and expensive to maintain. If anything is worn or looks suspicious, it must be repaired or replaced.

St. Agatha's is a small parish and is not rich, but the buildings and grounds are well maintained and thieves may be attracted to it.

All of these things must be done each spring, so what was to have been a wonderful, restful and relaxing time turned out to be as busy as ever. But then something happened in an unpleasant place.

Close to the rectory is a little grocery store. It is never clean and is not a very safe place to shop. Sometimes, however, when I am short on time, I do go there.

One day while I was standing in line in the store, I noticed a pleasant middle-aged man whom I thought might be a military man. He was standing behind me at the checkout counter. I saw a miniature silver eagle on his lapel, and I smiled at him. We introduced ourselves and began talking. As we talked, I listened to this man's unhappy Catholic voice.

The man seemed to be bitter and said that the Church must return to its traditions, and he asked me to pray that the Church will not become too liberal.

"The pope works hard," I said. "The Holy Spirit will work through him to protect the Church. History shows us that it is not Divinity but humanity that is flawed, and the Church was also organized by people. Though people change through time, the Gospel prevails as the true teaching of our Lord."

The colonel, as I had discovered his title earlier, continued to express his frustrations with Vatican II. He asked me to help him come back to the Church because he felt lost and disappointed.

I reminded the colonel that the Church was not a military organization and that there was supposed to be love, compassion and prayer. The Church has prospered and has continued to spread Christ's message of love.

The colonel told me an experience he had while serving in Europe.

"When I went to Europe after World War II," he said, "I was impressed with the Polish soldiers I saw. History tells us that, with horses and swords, they met the German invaders with their tanks and planes. They were true heroes." He had tears in his eyes as he spoke.

"I salute you, Michael," he said when he found out my military background, "for being part of such a brave Polish army."

He then invited me to the Blue Eagle's Club to share some of my experiences as a Polish colonel and priest in America. The meeting was pleasant and I enjoyed visiting the Blue Eagle's Club. I feel that we should respect men in uniform. Thanks to them we are free.

On occasion an insurance representative comes to visit the rectory. Business is a business, and on this particular visit we needed a few hours to complete the necessary discussion. The gentleman asked if he could see the pastor, the janitor, the housekeeper, and the secretary. When I realized I would have to introduce them all, I laughed.

He was a very pleasant man who had worked for the diocese for many years. He commented on how clean and neat the place was and that it reminded him of his years when he had lived in an orphanage. We soon realized that being raised by nuns was something we had in common. We discussed our childhoods, both under the stern hand of the nuns in this country and in Poland.

Joe Smith, the insurance man, asked about seeing the janitor, so I took off my collar and moved to the left and moved to the right and said, "Here is the janitor."

We started to laugh. Then Joe asked to speak to the housekeeper. This time I went into the next room and answered in a falsetto voice, "There will be pierogi for dinner." And we laughed again.

Joe told me that, in all the years he had been visiting parishes, no one had asked him to have coffee and doughnuts. I told him that it is a Slavic custom to treat strangers to hospitality and friendliness.

Another time, I was looking for someone to come to repair the parking lots and roofs. After receiving several exorbitant estimates, I decided to look for the Amish gentleman who did work with concrete and bricks and was known for his honesty.

I went where so many Amish live and ended up at the flea market which was in progress that day. I hoped that I would find someone who could tell me about the man and where he lived.

As I looked through the stalls, I heard someone calling my name. I looked around and saw a retired professor from the Modern Language Department from the University of Richton. He was selling produce with his son.

I mentioned to him why I was there and was pleased to find out that my friend knew the gentleman that I sought. His name was Noah York.

Mr. York promised to help me find someone to do the work. As I drove home, I was happy that I was able to find someone to do the badly needed work around the church and rectory.

Again I am reminded that there are both moments of achievement and joy, as well as moments of sadness, but if we have graces from God and numerous friends surrounding us, we can get over difficulties much easier. Without friends, life is sad.

Sometimes even those who are not especially friends make us smile because they are interested in what goes on in the church, even though they do not necessarily take an active role in the activities of the parish life. Such a person is Martha Unum. She is somewhat of a contradiction. She wears contemporary glasses and a babushka. Some of her questions surprise me, but they give me an idea of how lay people who are not involved in pastoral ministry are still interested in what happens.

During Lent and close to the Holy Week, Martha approached me, this time dressed in a brightly flowered dress, a green jacket and a hat with a feather on it. I smiled at the change from the babushka to an Irish colored hat. It was St. Patrick's Day and she wanted to look Irish, although she speaks English with a Polish accent.

"Are you going to have nice flowers this year?" she asked. "Be sure the church is clean and get busy with the preparations. I plan to attend some Holy Week celebrations."

"Thanks, Martha, for being concerned with the preparations," I responded.

I am truly grateful that there are people who are more helpful than Martha. Many are so willing to give of themselves and their talents to the church.

There is a greenhouse located close to the church, where there are friendly Christian people who for years have welcomed and helped me. Kathleen Dory, who works at the flower shop, knows how many flowers I want and orders the best lilies and azaleas for me.

But there is another preparation that takes place at this time. It is a spiritual renewal of meditation and lamentation at the Stations of the Cross. It is a good preparation for the Sacrament of Penance. I encourage everyone to attend the devotions and to make a good confession. I point out that we are not so holy that we do not need to apologize to God for our sins. I also point out that our Lord is a kind and forgiving Father for all His children who come to ask for forgiveness.

I like to point out that Jesus had great compassion and kindness for everyone, even for the worst sinners. In the Gospel, He defended the woman who was about to be stoned by her contemporaries and did not condemn her. He gives us a good example, that we should not condemn, but help all people to be reconciled with God.

Corpus Christi is another feast which requires preparation. Parishioners donate flowers from their gardens to decorate the altars where the Blessed Sacrament is exposed for adoration. We sing religious songs and hymns, and the music is so lovely. The organist, who is not Polish, plays the hymns beautifully and follows the liturgy so well.

The sound of organs and choirs lifts up my heart as a way of praising Almighty God and the saints in Heaven. It would be a sad, empty church without music for masses and funerals and weddings. Music inspires the priests and the parishioners alike in their quest for religious truths.

Celebrations of Christmas and Easter are festivities central to the Christian faith. It reminds the human heart and mind to return again and again to the origin of our faith which we find in the Nativity and the Resurrection.

God sent His son to make us partners in His creation through His divine nature. The finest gift is the realization that, after our death, we continue to live forever in the presence of Almighty God and His saints and angels.

Sometimes I mention this in my sermons. Not only those who were canonized are saints, but saints are also our family and friends who have been rewarded with happiness and joy in Heaven. Saints are declared on earth and found in Heaven. There is always a struggle to be virtuous and saintly by trying over and over again to make progress toward eternal happiness, and I say that it is possible to achieve such happiness.

When we celebrate Christmas, we adore a newborn baby who is man and God, but we also wonder why a Messiah who was prophetized for ages was not well accepted by all mankind. It is difficult to satisfy the human heart. When He arrived, many did not accept His gentleness and compassion. The people were looking for a general to defeat the conquerors because they were enslaved and occupied by enemies. But, in spite of this, Jesus was still gentle and loving.

I do not want to share with my flock a complicated theological interpretation. While I preach, I simply encourage the people to develop a love for the great gift of life from God. He offers an opportunity to reconcile with Him. Before the Alleluia was sung in Heaven, Jesus proclaimed the Gospel, set guidelines for organizing the Church, and left Himself at the Last Supper to be with us in the Holy Eucharist.

The center of Christian Catholic life is the presence of our Lord in the Tabernaculum, where he awaits our invitation into our hearts. This is a very important doctrine of our Church. The very core of this celebration is the Passion of our Lord. Why did He give Himself to be humiliated? Why did Jesus have to be crucified instead of Barabas, a well known criminal? Where were the witnesses to Jesus' miracles? What happened to St. Peter that he denied our Lord? We often ask these questions.

But the Virgin Mary and the other women stayed close to Him. She knew her son had the divine nature of God. The human nature of her son suffered the pain of rejection and physical torture and death. But His victory and glory came when He was raised from the dead.

All mankind can know that He was God. He stayed with the apostles for forty days after His Resurrection to organize His Church on earth. He told them again and again to teach what He had taught them, to proclaim His Gospel to all nations.

Furthermore, I realize that this is not only a commemoration of our Lord's Resurrection, but a preparation for Heaven, the hope for forgiveness of sins, and reward for commitment of God and to the people of God.

Holy Saturday is a traditional day of sharing food when I bless the Easter baskets in the Slavic style. The people bring sausage, ham, and other goodies to be blessed, and they often share some with me. I am happy to have some good food to eat for Easter.

After the last mass on Easter, I was very tired. But after closing the church and performing other sacristan duties, I was happy that the celebrations had been attended by so many people. The people sang to the organ accompaniment, and readings by the lecturers were beautiful. Everyone was friendly and warm, and I felt good. Finally I felt fulfilled that I was a servant of God and of the Church.

The day after Easter when I thought I could rest, something unusual happened. I came home from the university to find a message from Martha Adams on the answering machine. Martha is not a parishioner, but she wanted to meet with me for about fifteen minutes. I agreed to see her.

When she arrived for her appointment, she had a child with her that reminded me of a little devil. She didn't say hello, but just screamed and scratched the furniture.

"I'm giving you just fifteen minutes to baptize this child," said Martha. "I want her to be baptized without her parents knowledge, no witnesses and no records."

"It's impossible!" I said.

"It's possible; you just bring the Holy Water and do it right this minute," she demanded.

"Martha, please! The law of the Church forbids this. There must be godparents, and the parents must be informed and be instructed and give their permission," I told her.

"What instructions? Does the Church push people away?"

"I belong to the bishop. I obey Church law," I replied.

Martha retorted, "I will tell no one! If you will not do this, I will tell you to go to hell!"

Her babushka was falling down on her face; her glasses were smudged, and she looked so pathetic.

"But I must follow the rules… "

"Don't give me that. You have five minutes left."

But there was no negotiation. I insisted on meeting with the parents and to have their approval that the child be baptized and registered.

Martha was so upset that she pounded her fists on the table. "The Church and bishops are pushing people away. I'll find another priest," she said.

At last Martha gave up and slammed the door as she left.

I never saw Martha or the child again, but I often think of the child and wonder how she is doing. Has she found the blessings of God, the Church and prayer?

There is always a need for prayer. Without prayers or a feeling of the presence of Jesus in our daily lives, a person's life would be less meaningful and more lonely and depressing.

Of course there are ups and downs in the life of a small parish priest. The spiritual life can be disturbed by one's own weaknesses or those of the secular world and by materialism which does not satisfy the heart completely.

I remember when my friend, Bishop George Gilbride, told me that education has more value than American dollars.

He said, "You can earn the dollars, but you may lose them. Education stays with you as long as you live. You will always benefit."

2

Assessing the Past and the Present in Pastoral Ministry

Through reflections, descriptions, discussions and meetings with friends, there is in this chapter an assessment of Father Michael's pastoral ministry.

There are many benefits that I have from the people in the parish. People often show their affection for me by offering a mass for my health and blessing or taking me out to dinner, especially for my birthday.

One of my friends thought I needed companionship, so on my birthdays and for Christmas I receive teddy bears, which watch my sleep and protect me. The teddy bear collection still grows. I am thankful for so many friends who support me with kindness and with prayers.

It took a long time for the parish council and me to organize the parish, but now it is comfortable. The growing trees and flowers remind me how time passes and how great God is who shows His presence and protection through the wonders of nature and through good people.

The gazebo was built in the midst of the pine trees in the back of the church. It provides shelter after I have cut the grass and is also a good place for me to sit and meditate as I am doing now. It protects me from the rain. There is a small shrine to St. Jude, my patron saint whom I trust and from whom I receive help. I believe that St. Jude helps me do impossible things to satisfy my commitment and to serve the parish, which needs spiritual guidance, work, attention, and repair.

One summer while I attended a retreat, I met Father Jon O'Brien. He was a dynamic priest from someplace in the sunshine state of Florida. He had once served in the same diocese as I do. He moved from Ohio because of poor health. His doctor had advised him to change climates, but he also moved because of his depression.

Father O'Brien wrote to me occasionally after our meeting at the retreat. I knew that he was involved in the Pentecost movement in the Church and that he also loved his pastoral duties among the youths and young adults. He had also done research on the problems of stress among the clergy.

While he was visiting relatives here, he stopped to talk. I figured that his visit was a coincidence. However, a week earlier there had been an article in the paper about stress among the clergy. The two of us had a lengthy discussion regarding this troubling matter.

While we were talking, he asked me how I was doing and how my work schedule was. He then asked me when I had last had a vacation. I said that I didn't like to talk about it, but in honesty, my last vacation was over twenty years ago, before my appointment as pastor of St. Agatha's. I really had planned to go visit friends in Ottawa, Canada, but had to change my plans at the last minute. It seems that I always need to do something else more important, and then time just flies by and I do not get a vacation.

Father O'Brien told me that it was unhealthy not to change my environment from time to time. He even said that he considered it a mortal sin because I was killing myself.

I tried to explain to him that I had to stay for a variety of reasons. Even when I left for a short time to work on my thesis, I came back to a big surprise.

Once while I was gone, a priest who came from Europe was willing to substitute for me, but I soon discovered that he had tried to replace me in the parish. And there was another time that I was gone and a religious priest from Poland agreed to take over my duties for a time. He wanted to make St. Agatha's a center for other priests and brothers so that they could come to the United States. I came back and found that I had almost lost my parish. That priest's idea was most certainly not to help the parishioners, but to help the people who were coming from Poland.

Another and a very important reason that I do not get many vacations is that there is a shortage of priests, so there really isn't anyone to perform my duties while I am gone.

Father O'Brien sat down and started to lecture. "Remember when we promised to be friends?" he asked. "Let's talk like friends. If we don't eat properly, exercise, or rest enough and work too much, we burn out."

I remembered reading about this in the newspaper and told Father O'Brien about it.

"There are too many things to remember. Stress will shorten a person's life," he continued.

"Well, I went to see my doctor after a long time. He discovered my problem and he gave me some medicine for my stomach. It helps. But you are right, I know that I must avoid stress and take your advice," I said.

My friend left with an offer to allow me to use his condominium in Florida. All I had to do was let him know when I was coming. I thanked Father O'Brien for his kind invitation, but I knew that I would probably never make the trip to that warm state. I will, however, try to exercise more; maybe I will go swimming or running.

Later, as I was browsing through a Catholic book store, I saw a book titled *Priests and Stress*, published by the American Bishop's Conference. It contained the same advice that Father O'Brien had given me.

After reading the book, I called Father O'Brien and told him that he was right, that the bishops are worried about us and they do encourage us to be sensible. They advise us not to lose the image of ourselves as human beings in our ministry. At least I had begun to think about the seriousness of stress in my life.

Some time later I went for a walk around the neighborhood and I thought about how the times had changed. It was good that the bishops cared about us and gave us advice. When I was ordained, they expected nothing but sacrifice and more sacrifice. I understood that to mean that I had only to work until I became burned out and then reap my reward in Heaven. Now I observed that there is a better relationship between priests and bishops. They no longer seem to show absolute power; they now are willing to listen and to offer help.

One of my friends became the bishop of the diocese of Hopeland. This handsome Italian priest has stressed in his sermons that he is always willing to listen to the problems of the clergy and to help with respect and compassion.

Occasionally it is healthy to think about what we are doing to our lives. We must remember to think of ourselves, as well as others. Meditation and reflection help us. There is much about God's attributes that we need to think about the goodness that people share with us.

I did not realize how fast time passes until someone asked me how old I am now. Even the children from C.C.D. classes want to know.

"How old are you, Father Michael?" asked Chris Adams.

"In America we don't tell our ages," I answered.

So the children began to guess my age. Joyce Adams thought I was twenty-seven, but another child said that I must be at least seventy-five years old.

I didn't smile at that remark, but when class was over, I walked from my desk ever so slowly.

"See," said the child, "he must be older than seventy-five years."

I am not really worried about growing old because my mind is still active and I am still very busy. I still have a lot of ideas and goals to fulfill and some projects to complete.

One day a distant cousin surprised me when she asked me who would pay for my funeral when I died—the diocese, parish, or who?

It was the second time someone had asked me who would pay for my funeral. When I had surgery, my aunt, Magdalena Urycki, also asked me who would pay for my funeral. This time I just smiled and said that it would be taken care of, but these comments really hurt.

Before saying mass one morning, I looked out the window and saw that it was raining again. I knew that it would be difficult to work outside that day, but I also knew that the yard work cannot be neglected. As always in the spring, trees needed to be trimmed and flower beds readied for plants, but I knew I would not be able to do it that day.

Later I went to church to say mass as usual. There were only a few people there, and one of them was a small boy. It was Timothy Arthur, who is an intelligent, outspoken three year old. He stopped at the sacristy, and when he knocked on the door, I answered by knocking on the other side of the door. He opened it and we shook hands, and then he started to complain that I had put out the candles after mass instead of letting him do it. Timothy said that he wanted to do it himself for Jesus.

I said to him, "Sorry, I'll let you put out the candles if you help me take out the garbage sometimes."

"No, I don't have time," replied Timothy.

"Why can't you help me now? What are you doing today?"

"Oh, I'm helping my mother do the laundry, so you see I can't help you with the garbage."

This same child and his one year old brother sometimes scream and cry while I try to say mass, but I think it is good for children to come to church. It gets them off to a good start.

34

As I returned to the rectory, I stopped to look around the yard. It had rained for many days, and the flowers did not look happy. They were drooping because the ground was saturated with water. The grass needed to be cut, but it was too wet to do so. It didn't look hopeful that it would turn into a sunny day.

Because I could not work outside, I watched television. I switched channels often, but finally settled on an interview with a writer who had done some research and had, of course, published a book about how America was number one in many ways.

As I watched, I began to think. I wondered what was so important about being *number one*. I thought about this country's greatness and told myself that we are a very powerful nation, but at the same time, though we are, we do not know what to do about all the weapons that are stockpiled throughout the country.

As I sat there pondering America's wonderful assets, I thought that its greatness is somehow overshadowed by the deterioration of family life. Children are neglected because both parents work to provide housing, food, and simply to be able to pay the bills. The unity and strength of the family must be reinforced, and there must be help provided for the parents. Certainly, the help our country gives overseas could be channeled here at home.

I also believe that there is a shortage of religious leaders of all faiths in this world. It is because people do not want to commit themselves to God or to their country. I believe that religious institutions are valuable assets and that they provide moral guidance and teach respect for God and the law. Clergy remind us to do the best for God and to treat each other with respect. Because there are shortages of clergy, many churches close, so the moral teachings do not reach as many people. Without respect and love for our neighbors, even the greatest country will collapse.

I realize that prayer gives more hope and trust for heavenly help that our Lord will inspire young American boys to sacrifice their lives for God and become priests. I also believe that this solution— prayer—is more helpful and will be far more successful than any other solution.

As I sat in the gazebo, the wind blew around me, and I noticed the local religious newspaper lay before me. I looked at it, and I reflected on the many changes in the world. These changes that the paper discussed disturb me.

I think, "Why are there so many statistics here concerning Church problems?"

For instance, there is a new study out that finds younger priests are more conservative. The article compares the 1970s with the 1990s about the concerns of celibacy for priests and nuns. I question why these articles are published in the newspaper for the general public. What do these articles achieve?

They also state that only one in eight priests was questioned for the survey. What about the opinions of the other seven priests not questioned? I was not questioned about celibacy or if women should be ordained.

On the same table lay the *Catholic Digest*. A Protestant minister had written an article in which he urges Catholics to respect and to obey Church teachings and Church authority. He says that we should be proud of being very well organized under the leadership of our superiors.

I mention this, and in my simple way I believe that, instead of all the statistics and numbers, we should get down on our knees and ask God to bless the priests with long, happy and healthy lives. Maybe meditating in this manner is a better way for me to avoid getting upset over these articles. On the news media about this same time, a potential judge for the Supreme Court was being questioned by Congress. That day some Polish diplomats who were visiting in Richton stopped to have lunch with me. This nominated justice was being accused of sexual harassment, and it was being splashed all over the media. These diplomats saw this as very damaging for the whole country. They felt that garbage does not deserve this much attention. They also believe that the media should just keep quiet and stop generalizing and sensationalizing about people who are in the public eye. Perhaps they are right.

Later on I looked out over the church property and my mind wandered to very different topics. St. Agatha's is very fortunate to be in a city where young people have an opportunity to attend several universities. On an average the University of Richton has about thirty thousand students, and to the north is Tri-State University where over twenty thousand are enrolled. Both of these universities attract scholars from Poland to teach through an exchange program which can be for two or three years' duration.

Since most native Poles are Catholic and since there is only one Polish parish, they usually attend services at this parish. I recognize the native Poles when they come to church and am pleased to have them with us. They are enthusiastic and young, and many specialize in science and/or medicine. We often get together after church to share a little food and lots of discussion, since we are all part of the faculty of a university.

But there are some sad memories about them. One particular professor comes to mind. He brought his wife to this country to divorce her on the grounds of mental incompetence. Getting a divorce is much easier in America than in Poland. By the time they discovered that her problem was glandular rather than mental, his marriage had been destroyed and he was remarried to a Spanish woman. They had to be married outside the Church, and this saddened me very much.

There are happy moments, too. One of those occurred when Yolanda Gadanina, her husband Jan, and their son came to visit. We became good friends when they lived here while Jan worked in research in polymer science at the University of Richton. Once when they came to St. Agatha's, Yolanda fixed me tripe soup, one of my favorite dishes. I recall, as a student in Poland while traveling through Warsaw, I stopped at a restaurant where only fresh bread and tripe soup were served. Yolanda's soup reminded me of that time.

I have very fond memories of Yolanda, Jan and their son. When they decided to stay in the United States, I helped them get through all the paperwork at immigration. They no longer live in Ohio, but both are very successful scientists and Jan works in polymer.

Another very gifted and well-educated Polish man, Christopher Rose, lives in our community, too. He came to the United States as a refugee from the Polish Communist government and was sponsored by a local Christian church. Christopher is not fortunate enough to be able to work in his profession, which is physics. Now he does landscaping and is very good at what he does.

He is also a gifted and talented artist, and I enjoy looking at his work. He has decorated the church, the rectory, and the parish house with his paintings of flowers. His touch has enhanced the beauty of the rooms.

More and more people who come from Poland stay for only two or three years, but while they are here, we become friends. During these moments, we discuss the difficult times, as well as the glorious times, for Poland. We all share a common love for Poland and her culture. I learn what is happening in Poland from them, as the country changes from Communism to Democracy. There is a lot to admire about my fatherland, but I worry about the economic and political changes that are taking place because they seem to take place slower than anyone anticipated.

It is easier to work in a system where the rules are carefully defined for the people and punishment is severe and swift for any transgression. And now, along with the Western style of life, there is a big negative aspect of their society—an increase in crime in the bigger cities.

In some Eastern European countries, people can make a great deal of money very fast, mostly by being dishonest. Middle-class people cannot afford to buy the goods from the West that appear in their stores. They cannot afford medical treatment. The *zloty*— without great value—is devalued and everyone is a millionaire. The government is not stable and the president, who is the hero of the Solidarity movement, Lech Brave, is not educated enough nor prepared enough to act as a politician, but he has good intentions and he is honest.

It is obvious that it will be a long time before Poland is like other Western countries. People must make sacrifices and learn to think not only of themselves. When they worked for the Germans or the Communists, they didn't care, but now they must work for themselves to bring their country into the mainstream.

It shows us that we in the United States should appreciate what we have, and we should be grateful to God that we live here in this great country.

It is not something unusual at St. Agatha's to have guests from Washington. It reminds me of when I lived in Poland and we had visitors coming and going at the Church of St. Andrew in Mazury. When I was a young pastor, we had visitors from all walks of life, from the young bishop who would later become pope to mine workers. Everyone came to Mazury to fish and to relax on the shores of the beautiful lakes.

Many of them, especially the priests, stopped at the rectory to pay me a visit. But that is all in the past.

Now, because of my promotion to colonel in the Polish army, I have gained the attention of the Polish government. When the general consul, Jerry Kwiatek, passes through Richton, he stops and stays with me for a while. There are also people who work for the Polish embassy who come occasionally.

At first I wondered if I had anything in common with them. I have been away from Poland for many, many years, and I felt a little vulnerable because of the way the Polish government treated its clergy over the last forty years.

However, I felt hospitable and generous toward them, and they have become friends, especially Colonel Bogdan Pilot and his family. When they visited me, they were so kind and brought me souvenirs, including some pure Polish vodka. We spent several days visiting and talking about Poland's history and the way the country is now. When they left, I missed their company. We keep in touch with an occasional letter or call. I remember when Colonel Bogdan and I attended a promotion ceremony at the University of Richton for a lieutenant and the red and white roses the colonel presented to the lieutenant's wife.

At another time when Colonel Bogdan, an air force pilot, and I were guests of Colonel Russell May of the University of Richton in the Military Science Department, Colonels May and Bogdan exchanged memories and Colonel Bogdan had tears in his eyes when he thought about the changes in the relationship between Poland and the United States. Something else is important concerning these two countries. I learned that the Polish cadets are being invited to train at the military academies such as West Point.

Leaving the university, Colonel Bogdan Pilot expressed his gratitude for the opportunity to visit the department and to talk with other military men. In the corridor, he noticed the picture of the secretary of defense of the United States and General Colin Powell, whom he had had the opportunity to meet at the Polish embassy in Washington.

After this pleasant visit, I went back to the everyday problems in the community. For a while the neighborhood was quiet, but one day some detectives approached me and asked me to do something about the parish's garbage bin. They said that they were informed that someone was using the dumpster for a drop-off for drugs. I asked them what I should do about the problem. They suggested that I ask the sanitation company to install a new dumpster which had a lock on it. It seems to have worked as we have had no problem since.

After the drug incident, I saw something strange happen. A little girl, about eleven, started to paint graffiti on the fence across from the church. It was after the parking lot and the wall of the church had been repaired and painted. She started with water, but that didn't seem to satisfy her artistic talents. She looked for someplace to decorate with the pink paint she had hidden in the shrubbery nearby, but I found it first. I went to her house and took the paint with me. I asked her mother to please tell her daughter to stop painting graffiti because I didn't want her to deface property. The woman was terribly upset and used vulgar language and swore unlike any man I had ever heard. I was surprised that the woman reacted in that way. I felt that I had no choice but to call the police. When they arrived, together we were able to calm the woman down. I felt terrible about the situation, but I work hard to keep up the property and cannot understand why people want to destroy it.

One Sunday as I was unlocking the gate to the church, I looked across the street. The people who lived there had been arrested several times, and on several occasions when they saw me, they made obscene gestures toward me for no apparent reason. On this particular day, I decided to speak to the man who was leaving the house. I asked him to please ask his friends not to disturb me when I come to open the church. The man said that he would try to help rectify the situation, and for a while it was better.

From these unpleasant situations I began to meditate on the administration of the parish.

One day as I awaited the arrival of a friend, Consul Wieslaw Urbanek, who was arriving to visit on his way to New York, I decided to do a few things around the property. After mass, I went to look at the garage. Behind it are some wild bushes that send roots and branches into the ventilation of the garage. I decided to take a ladder and clippers and climb onto the roof. All the spoutings were full of rotten leaves, dead birds, and old toys tossed up there by the neighborhood children. Looking at this mess, I realized it was time to clean out the spouting, throw everything away so that water could drain more easily from the roof. I trimmed the bushes growing near the roof and cut the branches into little pieces. I brought an old white sheet from the rectory and carried the debris from the roof to the dumpster. As I worked, a man stopped and asked me what I was doing. He said that I looked funny carrying that strange bundle on my back.

"Take my advice and don't work so hard," he said as he drank from his bottle of wine, and then he ambled his way down the street.

I stopped him and asked if he was working anywhere.

"I don't have to work," the man replied. "You work for me by paying your taxes."

I decided to forgo any further discussion with this man. I thought how sad it is that such a young man, not more than twenty-five or six, should be so lazy and without goals in his life. When I meet people like this, I find it difficult to believe that they do not care to achieve anything in life. After so many years in the same place, I realize that there seems to be more and more people like this young man, and it troubles me.

As I went back to my work, I heard someone call to me from the parking lot. It was a young parishioner who comes to mass every day. She had two children and one on the way. She was disturbed by the people who talk in the church when she tries to meditate.

"You should tell them to be quiet in the church. Aren't you the priest?" she asked.

What this woman doesn't understand is that many of these people are older and have become hard of hearing. Many are retired, and when they come to church, they want to talk to each other. I understand that, even though the church is a holy place, these older people just will not change. On the other hand, when she brings her children to mass every day, they scream and cry and play in the center aisle. She obviously does not see her own children as she complains about the older women. I am happy when I hear the birds sing through the church's open windows as these people praise God. When things get too complicated, I try to smile and to realize that it is all a part of human nature. I know that, under the babushkas and in the hearts of children, there is an innocence of a human being that is endearing to God.

The woman continued to complain as I worked on the roof of the garage. She said that she was disturbed because people in this country do not pay enough homage to the Virgin Mary.

"Something terrible will happen if there is no devotion to the Virgin Mary," she continued angrily. "Maybe our lives are too good."

I reminded her that in the Virgin Mary we have an intercessor in Heaven. The Virgin Mary makes our churches homelike because our devotion to her reminds us of our mothers who took care of us and protected us against anyone who would hurt us or punish us. We need the Virgin Mary to protect us.

One morning after mass, even before I ate breakfast, I decided to cut the grass because it had grown so fast lately. But the lawn mower disobeyed me and wouldn't start. So before I could cut the grass, I had to fix the lawn mower. Before I began the actual mowing, I went to change my shoes and decided to wear the boots I wear when I ride my motorcycle. They are old, almost thirty years, but they are still in good condition. While I mowed, I saw many bottles along the front and side of the church property; I even found some pistol bullets which had been fired. As I continued, I found more trash, but this time I didn't pick it up but kicked it with my boots.

Over the years I have picked up many, many bags of trash, even some that was not on the church property, but nearby. This time, I decided to leave it and see how much would pile up before someone would clean it up.

I tried to forget this unpleasantness. When I got back to the rectory, I found a card from a woman whose sister had died and for whom I had conducted funeral services. In the card was a check for $100 as a donation to the church in memory of her sister. It helped to erase the bad feelings I had about people.

Some time later as I waited for the water for my tea to boil, I tried to find diversion on television, but since the presidential convention was being broadcast, there was only politics and more politics.

A few days after that occurred, two Polish consuls, Wieslaw and Christopher, would stop to visit. They would both wonder why there was so much money being spent on elections while, at the same time, the candidates slandered each other. They felt that it discouraged the people from voting.

"I have seen many presidential elections since coming to this country, and people always get pretty excited about them," I would tell them.

"Promises are made and broken, and everybody finds faults with everybody else. Eventually someone becomes president and we all survive, but the political situation is disturbing at best. And it is still two months before a president will be elected."

It is sad that issues such as abortion, crime, international politics, and poverty are so important that they have such an effect on an election.

Finally, I decided to give up watching the candidates on television and go to finish the laundry. I also had work to do before school started.

Sometimes I wonder about the many things in life which are not pleasant, but I believe one of the important elements in our lives is prayer—our strength.

So much can be said about prayer. It is a simple way to define our communication with God, the Almighty, our Creator. How often do we concentrate on the attributes of the forgiving, merciful Father?

It is impossible to live a religious life without prayer. Prayer is essential to a priestly life. Prayer begins in the morning to establish communication and to acknowledge the presence of God. It is the realization that we are called by God to serve for man's salvation.

In the form of mass every day, strength comes through prayer. A priest realizes how privileged he is to repeat the words that were inspired by God and written by great prophets, religious leaders, popes, martyrs, and confessors. There is the acknowledgment that we are nothing compared to the greatness of our Lord. He calls us to His ministry, and He cares about us.

We acknowledge that a royal priesthood, created by God and mentioned by St. Paul, will give eternal salvation for those who commit themselves to God.

One example of a longing prayer for God is Psalm 63:1–4:

O God, you are my God whom I seek; for you my flesh pines and my soul thirsts like the earth, parched, lifeless and without water. Thus have I gazed toward you in the sanctuary to see your power and your glory, for kindness is a greater good than life; my lips shall glorify you.

This psalm ends one of the morning prayers for a priest. Perhaps the evening prayer is best, Psalm 139:1–3, 23–24:

O Lord, you have probed me and you know me, you know when I sit and when I stand; you understand my thoughts from afar. My journeys and my rest you scrutinize, with all my ways you are familiar... Probe me, O God, and know my heart; try me, and know my thoughts. See if my way is crooked, and lead me in the way of old.

It is almost impossible to write all the beautiful readings and meditations to be found in the priestly Breviary because there are four volumes of everyday prayers.

Besides the Breviary, I like to read the history of the Church. There I discovered that many clergy and secular educators have received many blessings from Jesus in His work, just as He promised, and that the apostles understood that Jesus meant for the Church to be strong and that nothing would destroy it. History has proven this to be true.

The Catholic Church has thrived down through the ages under the care of Divine Providence. Despite adversaries, the faithful have continued to acknowledge Christ as their Lord. They gathered secretly to celebrate the Holy Eucharist and were ready to die for Him. Did they question? Yes. But did they prosper in holiness? Yes. Many Christians achieved high levels of holiness and were recognized and canonized as saints of the Church.

I do not consider myself a saint, but I praise God for the strength I need to help His Church. I feel the best when I am saying mass and administering the Sacraments. I have faith that the merciful God will reward me for my efforts and commitment by making a little space in Heaven where I can rest and enjoy eternal happiness.

However, sometimes there is nothing that can be done to stop some uncomfortable situations in the life of a priest. Often, people take advantage of a parish or the good nature of the pastor. Often, salespeople come trying to sell their products. They are persistent, and even if it is something that the parish does not need, they still continue to try to sell. But it is very difficult for me to say no because I always want to help people.

I recall one such incident when the roof and the parking lot had to be checked for repairs. According to the Diocesan Financial and Legal Office, three companies had to submit bids for the work. When the prices came in, the difference among the quotes was very great. Naturally, it was necessary that the job go to the lowest bidder.

Later I was in a restaurant when I was approached by one of the businessmen who had submitted a proposal. He apparently wanted to embarrass me because he saw that I was with the deputy mayor and the city prosecutor and other friends from the city of Richton.

He said, "So, you didn't give me the roof job. Who was so lucky to take your parish money for fixing the church roof?"

I just smiled and told him that it was necessary that the church take the best price for the job.

Another difficult thing for me to do is to watch constantly the people who do the repairs. I often help them and even try to please them by bringing them doughnuts and soft drinks, but I still almost have to beg them to do the work properly. Sometimes the workers do not come on time, or they miss days, weeks, and months between working on the projects. The best way to get good workers is to ask friends. That is what I did when we needed to install a new fence because the old one became deteriorated. These friends gave me the telephone number of a reliable company, and the fence was up in a hurry.

I remember times when properties did not need to be fenced in. But it now protects the church property and keeps away people who not only park their cars on the lawn, but who drink alcoholic drinks and use the property to sell drugs. I feel like screaming and saying, "God help us in this country."

What is so terrible about this is the deprivation of character when little children can make $100 and even much more a day selling cocaine. How will this same child, in the future, work for wages that are only $2000 to $3000 a month?

Even though seeing these children in such deplorable situations, there are other sad tasks that I must perform. One is when I have to conduct a funeral for a parishioner. From the beginning of the priesthood, I remember different circumstances connected with funerals in different parishes.

As a young student of theology, I often spent my vacations near the city of Krakow. One day while I visited the local pastor, the cardinal of Krakow, Stephen Sapieha, arrived at the rectory to invite the pastor and me to the funeral of a priest who had been beheaded while saying his prayers in his home. A communist policeman had gone out of his mind and had attacked the priest. The window was open, and there had been no one there except the priest; the man entered through the open window and killed him.

I was very happy to see His Eminence Stephen Sapieha at the door, and in the traditional manner of the Church, I genuflected before the cardinal and kissed his ring. He was dressed in red, different from the parish priests. He smiled and responded to my greeting; we then went to the car to go to the very sad funeral.

On many other occasions I heard about several priests who were executed in concentration camps. This makes me unhappy to think that there was no respect for the Church.

There have been very painful and unpleasant experiences when I have visited funeral homes. Sometimes people, especially in the United States, who go to the funeral home to pay their last respects, do not pray. They should be paying homage in silence to the deceased instead of talking loudly and laughing during the time I am trying to say the Rosary with the bereaved.

There are other situations when, as much as I wanted to visit and bring Holy Communion to sick people, some members of the family were not in favor of this. I could see that they did not want me there, but I also tried to understand the selfishness of the family member who was in charge of the sick or dying person. They were not thinking of the person who was sick or dying, but perhaps of what they would gain. I still would go to visit a sick person or go to a funeral home to pray or to say good-bye to my parishioner, even though I was not invited.

Even the unhappy times are offset by successes. I felt very pleased when I had my two books of poetry published. They are entitled *The Beauty of Creation* and *A Touch of Divinity*. Since I was fourteen, I have written poetry, and some of the early ones were included in these collections. I do not pretend to be a poet; I just try the best that I can to express my gratitude to God and the people of God. Thanks to many of my friends, I became what I am, a priest of Christ and servant of the people for whom I have committed my life, my talents, and my ability.

Shortly after the poetry books were published, I sent copies to my Polish friend, Bogdan. He called to discuss the books, and I asked him for his opinion.

"Father Michael, you should continue to write. We all read your book of poems, and we expect that you will write more books," he said.

I asked him what he most liked, and he said, "The spiritual encouragement in our daily lives were reflected in these books." He continued that he, his family, and friends were inspired by my work and that I should continue to write. His remarks made me feel very good.

Upon occasion I believe that we have to experience situations that are depressing. It is impossible for a parish priest to ignore what is going on in a country such as the United States where, economically and politically, we are not in the best shape. These situations affect the individual lives of my parishioners.

I often ask many questions about these problems, but do not seem to get answers to many of them. Why are so many people without jobs? Some have never worked; some did, but do not do so now. It is strange; somehow these people eat and have a place to live, yet they do not work. I know that mostly the middle class of Americans work hard to pay taxes to support these people. I really want to encourage the younger people not to count on welfare, but to get an education and to get a good job.

While I meditated on this critical situation, I looked out the window and saw children riding like crazy on bicycles. This is very dangerous, since drivers often speed down the street at extremely high speeds even though it is posted for 25. I also was afraid that the children would damage the statue of our Lady, the Virgin Mother of God, which stands in front of the church. I ran from the rectory to check what was going on, and what I worried about had happened. The newly laid concrete had red and black lines from the tires of the bicycles.

I stopped the children and said, "Please, don't destroy what we just built for your convenience, and don't ride your bikes so fast here since traffic signs are not observed and you could get hurt. You may also destroy what we did in order to make it look better, not only for you, but also for a nice, clean and neat looking place for our neighborhood."

"Yes, Father," they said.

They left, riding their bikes up the street where they had come from. Hopefully, they will remember what was relayed to them and not cause any further destruction or damage to this beautiful area in front of St. Agatha's Church.

As I wandered back to the rectory, I began to think about my friends from the Polish embassy in Washington, D.C., and the consulate in New York City. I remembered that they had invited me to visit them. Some time ago it was just impossible to contact any of the representatives of the Polish government because of their unfriendly attitude toward the clergy. Now, since the political situation has changed, I have met the general consul, Jerry, and the two consuls, Wieslaw and Christopher, from New York and also the deputy military attache from the Polish embassy in Washington, D.C.

I went to New York for a banquet at the Polish consulate because my friend Consul Wieslaw Urbanek finished his diplomatic service and was going back to Poland. Jerry Kwiatek, general consul, invited me to come and to say a few words and a prayer. I was so excited to be able to attend. It was like a dream come true. I was able to be in my Polish army chaplain's uniform. What a wonderful experience to be there for my friend and to be with other Polish officials.

For the occasion I said a prayer that I would like to share: "Almighty Father, thank you that you allowed me, your servant, who at this moment represents Polish immigrants in this beautiful city of New York, to thank you first, for such an opportunity that I am allowed today to pray to You for those who are trying very hard to help Poland, my native country, to do the best in the matter of progress in justice. Thank you for giving my native country freedom and independence, and please protect those who beautifully worked hard for Poland and its people. They work for making good progress toward democracy, and above all, I am asking you, Almighty God, bless Consul Wieslaw and his family and the other officials who are going back to Poland that they may be happy over there, healthy, and continue to gain such popularity throughout their commitment and sacrifices which they show and deserve on this land. Amen."

When I finished this prayer, I added a little more. I said, "I can't get over the reality of today that I am with you, my dear Polish brothers and sisters. We have so much in common. In spite of living over thirty years in this country which I adopted as my own, and believe me, the beginning wasn't too easy, as you know from listening to somebody else, I was lucky that God blessed me and the other immigrants with health and heavenly help to do our best. Therefore, you could say that we are successful in our lives. We achieved a lot of things. Thanks to this political system that gave us equal opportunity to make progress in our lives. In spite of everything, we still, after living so many years in this country, use our hearts, minds and memories in wondering about the places where we were born and, perhaps, even from time to time, miss.

"For this beautiful occasion when we say good-bye to some of you, I wish to make some remarks simply to tell you that you gained our hearts. Your friendliness, gentleness, and because you care, make our feelings different so that we believe that, with such nice people like General Consul, His Excellency Jerry Kwiatek, and his wife Dr. Stanislawa, and the family of Consul Wieslaw, you brought a lot of happiness.

"On your assignment, may God bless you always, and believe me, you will not be forgotten for what you did in this crucial transitional changing in the beautiful country of Poland and also in all the Eastern European countries by building up a better relationship between Poland and the American people."

So it is not enough that I am involved in the spiritual leadership of my parish, but I am also well equipped to perform my ministry to military personnel. It makes me happy that I am welcomed to the Army R.O.T.C. as a chaplain.

Once, as a chaplain, I had the opportunity to meet with some American army generals. How was it that a veteran of the Second World War had such a great privilege? Well, one afternoon after I said my prayers, I lay down to rest and to watch television. As I watched the TV news, the president of the United States came into view ready to make an announcement about his nominee for the chairman of the Joint Chiefs of Staff, the man who would replace General Colin Powell. Even though I was exhausted, I sat up and paid attention when it was said that this gentleman, born in Poland and still with a slight Polish accent, was the nominee. What a surprise!

First, I prayed that the general would quickly be approved. Next, I contacted my commander, Major Don Algoode, and we both decided to send letters of congratulations to the general in the names of the cadets, officers, and staff of the R.O.T.C. of the University of Richton. Angelina, president of the parish council at St. Agatha's, sent a congratulatory letter, too. As a result we each received a lovely reply from the general.

I suppose one could wonder why I and the parish would be so concerned with this appointment. The answer is really quite simple. The parish council, the people of the parish, and I are all proud of this gentleman's Polish heritage. I also have very special feelings because we are both from Warsaw, Poland.

For Christmas I sent the general my newest book of poems, *America, Quo Vadis?*, and my greetings. I also said that I hoped that Major Algoode and I might have the opportunity to meet him in person and be able to shake his hand. The response from the general was positive, and he, in spite of being very busy, gave us the phone number of his secretary so we could call to make arrangements to see him if we were in Washington.

Shortly after Christmas, Major Algoode and I did have the opportunity to visit the Pentagon. We visited Chaplain Mark Ashe, a lieutenant colonel and chaplain of the United States Army. This kind man made it possible for us to meet the chief chaplain and the deputy chaplain of the Army, Joe Marni, a major general, and John Dubler, a brigadier general.

The visit was cordial and above all, after a salute to the general, I, as colonel chaplain, got a very warm reception from the chief chaplain and a recognition medal for my bishop. He also thanked me for serving the United States Army as a chaplain.

Finally, as we were leaving, the general gave me a big hug good-bye.

"General, sir, I really appreciate your kindness. Never in my life have I been hugged by a general. Thank you for showing your affection," I said.

I realized that the hug was for my commitment to the service of the United States Army.

Later that evening, Major Don Algoode and I were invited by the Polish embassy, Military Attache Colonel Marian, and his lovely wife, Irene, to dinner. We ate a delicious meal of Polish dishes.

After our visit was complete, we left Washington very happy. I have many pleasant memories of our time there.

This wonderful experience reminded me of the fine officers and commanders in the Polish underground that I met while I was still in Poland. They were good and kind men who wanted to help their country. This took a great deal of bravery on their parts.

When the changes took place in Poland, I met several other Polish officers who were also diplomats. We were able to meet several times, and these men were friendly and considerate.

Two of these Polish diplomats were General Tadeusz Dobry and Colonel Chaplain Tadeusz Mily. General Dobry, a man with a gentle disposition, belonged to the Polish government-in-exile.

I still say mass for him and his family sometimes. When World War II began, the general was a young officer. After catastrophe struck Europe during the German occupation, he worked for the Polish government and the defense ministry. However, he now lives in Chicago and represented the Polish government to the United States, Canada, and Mexico.

Besides the high ranking officers, there are two chaplains that I admire. One is Lieutenant Colonel Mark, at the chaplaincy head-quarters in the Pentagon. He helped Poland establish a chaplaincy policy which was sent through me to the bishop who is chief of Polish chaplains. The goal was to deal with soldiers from different religious backgrounds and to tell how to provide service by Catholic chaplains.

The other is Chaplain Tadeusz Mily, a colonel in the army and pastor of a military cathedral in Warsaw where the chaplaincy headquarters of Poland is located. We became acquainted through telephone conversations. We share a common commitment to provide service—the colonel to Polish soldiers and I to American soldiers.

There is no doubt that the brotherly atmosphere among the soldiers, subordination, and discipline did not only attract great sons and daughters of the United States, but also some clergy of different religious and various Christian denominations.

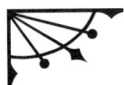

3

After God—Who?

Through faith, through study and through experience, Father Michael knows that friends are good instruments of a successful pastoral ministry. He also knows that, without friends, life could be sad. So, this chapter shows that friends, after God, are an excellent asset and that they not only do the best in Father Michael's life, but they also are cordial. There are those who cheer him up, and perhaps it is their friendship and encouragement that is the reason for his getting over the difficulties in his life and for achieving his goals.

I often ask myself what we would do without the help of friends. It is not enough, I think, to be ordained, to be educated, to be healthy, to be wise, to be committed to the pastoral, spiritual and earthly works, but there is also a need to have the help and blessing from God above all.

Second after God, friends are the important factor in the ministry. Pastors need friends who listen, advise, encourage, protect, and perhaps even to prevent something that would not be beneficial to the community. Fortunately, a priest's friends understand his vocation and commitment to the Church.

In the many years in the priesthood, I have met numerous good people in the parishes where I have worked, and as much as I tried not to be a bother to people, in many difficulties as well as in times of joy and achievement, my friends were with me. They are religious people with high morals, who are devoted to their families and their country. It often happens that they offer assistance and are able to share a friendship with their pastor, and as a result good things happen for the parish. For these good friends, I say a prayer of thanksgiving to God. Good friends are proof that God cares about us. Good deeds and activities show in their lives and that the presence of God is in them.

When I started my pastoral ministry in Poland, I had to build up friendships with my parishioners. I was very young when I became pastor at St. Andrew's in Mazury. There were many farmers and fishermen who were faithful and friendly. After long days of working with poor tools, equipment, and a lack of money, these poor farmers often shared what they had with me. Sometimes it was only dry bread, spoiled cheese and a glass of water, but it was always offered with kindness and sincerity. I have never forgotten them, and I pray for them. I know that many of these former friends are in Heaven, but still I pray for them.

After I left Poland and began my trip to America, on the ship I met a woman name Rose Pogodna. She was about seventy years old at that time. After we arrived, Rose introduced me to her family, which consisted of her son-in-law Frank Szydlo and her daughter Charlotte. For many years after that trip, these kind people invited me to stay with them while I was on vacation, and for twelve years

I was able to spend two weeks' vacation with these wonderful people. I had never dreamed of such things that they permitted me to use while I was there. They offered me their Cadillac sedan to drive and allowed me to use all of the home and recreational facilities. I have never forgotten these people.

Later, when I studied in Canada, I had the opportunity to become acquainted with nice Canadians who welcomed me with such friendship.

I experienced the most beautiful help from friends when I became the pastor at St. Agatha's parish. These friends really helped me to do my best, not only materially, but they supported the Church as well. Above all, they helped me spiritually when they encouraged me not to give up, but to do my best in some of the difficult times.

They were very generous, giving of their time by advising me, and even through physical work around the yard, in the school building, in the rectory, and in the parish house. I am sure that they did it for God and from their hearts. They still cheer up and support their pastor, especially now. I know that I cannot find any way to express my gratitude for all the friends who have helped me, but I pray and visit them and share their moments of joy and of sorrow.

I think it is good sometimes to have a day to help fight the everyday stress. It is especially important for a small parish priest to have some time to himself occasionally because of the many duties that he must perform. At times when I am under stress, I just like to stay home, especially when I have an evening mass. I don't have to get up early in the morning, open the church, and take care of all the necessities of the day. I just like to have a moment away from the outside world and to relax a little. It really helps me to work better and helps me to gain strength for my next duties.

Another way that is good to relax is to talk with friends who do not condemn me but understand and give advice. I often find, too, that reading is helpful. I recall a book, published by the National Conference of Catholic Bishops in 1981 on the subject of clergy stress, which gave a lot of good advice concerning the health of priests. The book suggested that priests should eat healthy food and get plenty of sleep, but I also believe that all of us should have goals in our lives and need to struggle to achieve them. Good exercise helps both the spiritual and physical growth.

So, while I was resting, I looked at my collection of books. "Oh, my God, when did I have time to read all those books," I thought to myself. I look at them and I remember chapters and important paragraphs. I know the color and condition of each one of the 3,500 books which I use for my classes in Slavic studies and religion. They are really my treasures.

One day as I looked for something in one of the books, I noticed the local religious newspaper lying on the table. I stopped for a moment to read an article on the editorial page which had been written by an ex-nun who had left the Church and married an ex-priest. These two were trying to come back into the pastoral ministry of the Church. "Oh, my God," I thought, "people who are bitter, upset, frustrated, and disappointed would not be successful in the pastoral ministry after years away from the service. Their world is different, their love is now different, and their commitment is contrary to when they were in the service of the Church years ago."

What concerns me the most is that the local religious paper publishes such unpleasant letters from ex-clergy who sometimes attack the pope and the hierarchy very openly when their request to return to the priesthood is not granted. I feel that the paper has gone far away from what should be its respect for the pope and the Church.

It seemed to me to be strange that the article by the ex-nun was given so much space, but when the bishop of Hopeland wrote about the shortage of priests, his article did not receive as much space. I was so upset that I wrote a letter explaining that I totally support the bishop and his brotherly approach toward the priests. My letter, however, was never published and another letter which criticized and attacked the Church was given a lot of space in the Roman Catholic newspaper.

Sometimes after a storm we experience beautiful weather. I learned this Polish proverb a long time ago and have found out how true it is.

Again it was time to get back to the book. I am always happy when a new semester begins. As I looked at my teaching aids, textbooks, quizzes, and organized syllabus, I knew that I was ready to go back to the classroom and to meet my new students. I thanked God for this great opportunity.

So I walked outside on the church property to check to see if everything was prepared for the fall season, or perhaps even for winter. As I looked around at everything, I knew that all was ready for the next two seasons. While I stood there, the mailman arrived. I greeted him politely and asked if he had something for me. He said that he had some letters and he hoped that they brought good news. I took the letters to the rectory to relax and read them. I noticed that one letter was from a lady whose husband had died a couple of years ago. I had helped him spiritually and had given him the last rites.

Usually we are sad when our friends leave us. We don't realize how much they mean to us and often take our friends for granted. It is even sadder if these friends have been instrumental in helping us to do our best.

The year 1992 started with farewells and departures of many friends. First my dear friend, President Robert Currey of the University of Richton, departed. It was indeed shocking news when another friend called one morning and said, "Your friend Robert Currey has accepted a new position as president of another university."

This same news was in the newspaper and on television. I did not believe that this could happen so soon, especially after this man had worked so hard to build up the reputation of the university.

Before Dr. Currey left, we met at the commissioning of officers for the air force and army. We shook hands and reminded each other that we would remain friends in spite of his moving away.

Over six hundred people stood in line to say good-bye at the farewell party given for Dr. and Mrs. Currey. It was a beautiful affair, although a sad one. Many people from the Modern Languages Department, including the chairman and I, attended. I was very sure that this would be the last time that I would see this couple. I did wish them well, and I told them that I would pray for them as they left for their new home.

While trying to cope with this situation, I was notified about the departure of the local bishop who had spent thirteen years helping to build a strong Church in this region. He kept the morale among the clergy, whom he called his co-workers in Jesus' vineyard. Following so closely upon the departure of Dr. Currey, I felt very sad to lose two such well respected people.

Thinking of the departure of my bishop, I remember a long time ago when he was in charge of diocesan missions. I met him when I came from Ottawa after finishing my graduate school. We met in front of St. John's Cathedral in Hopeland, Ohio. At the time, he was one of the diocesan directors and a very pleasant man. I did not realize that he, too, had a Polish background, and I was so happy when I learned that.

Later when I was appointed to St. Agatha's, this nice priest became an auxiliary bishop of Hopeland and general vicar for the region where my parish was located. His common sense and brotherly treatment of me was very welcomed. For his farewell and good-bye, I wished him the very best.

I soon learned that, at the pope's request, some auxiliary bishops around the world are being cut. Maybe it is because of the shortage of priests, but perhaps we need more parish priests than dignitaries. I am sure that only the pope knows why the region where I have a parish will not have a bishop anymore.

In spite of all the farewells, good-byes and sad feelings, life must go on. I am sure that God will provide the city, the university, and me with some good leaders.

At this same time something good was happening. The friendship among the college professors seemed to be deepening. I felt this when one said to me, "Listen, Father Michael, don't you leave, too." I suddenly began to feel closer to all of the members of the staff.

Later on there was one significant new event in the life of our parish. It was when Bishop Bernard O'Neill administered the Sacrament of Confirmation at St. Agatha's Church. After a great deal of preparation and a good response from the parishioners, the bishop was pleased with the good group of candidates for confirmation, and I was very happy, too.

From the pulpit I welcomed the bishop with the following remarks: "Dear Bishop, I remember and want to mention to my faithful people of St. Agatha's the moment I met you for the first time. It was over twenty-five years ago when I came from Europe. I stood in the middle of the chancery office waiting for the bishop, not being sure if I would be accepted into the diocese of Hopeland, Ohio, or if I would be rejected. Then I saw a young monsignor who looked at me and smiled. He could not speak Polish and I could not speak English, but then I knew I was accepted, not only in this country but to this diocese. That young monsignor was you. Thank you for your kindness, and thank you for your visit to our parish to administer the Sacrament of Confirmation. To welcome you, the people and I applaud you."

"Father Doctor Michael, you will be remembered for years because you grew and progressed in knowledge and in spiritual life," responded the bishop.

It was in the middle of the winter, and that evening the weather was terrible with heavy snow blowing hard. When everyone had gone and there were only the two of us, the bishop and the priest, we chatted as we sat in the recreation room of the rectory. Even though I was tired because of the celebration, I was glad and grateful to God that He had sent the bishop to cheer me up, as I missed the friends who had relocated.

It was difficult for me to get over this feeling quickly, but remembering my commitments helped. I began to realize that to be subordinate to authorities and to one's superiors is very important to me. Because of my background there have always been people who ruled over my life and to whom I had promised to obey.

This feeling of subordination started in early childhood when I was in the orphanage. Of course, devoted nuns with their habits, long veils, rosaries, and serious looking faces made me believe that being subordinate to others was a part of life, which it is. As a child, I was an excellent subject for this because of the nuns, priests, officers of the army, teachers, professors, deans of colleges, and bishops. But, it has not always been easy; sometimes it has been extremely difficult. It is something that has developed over the years.

This subordination to others has helped me as a priest. I know that I must obey God, and the people in my life who have taught me to obey helped me to see God's presence. Most of the authorities that I had to deal with had good intentions and gave me a good push to study and to teach me self discipline. All of these have helped me to set and to attain my goals. For them and what they taught me, I thank God each day.

Later, I stopped at the bishop's office to pick up a personal document that I had asked the bishop to prepare before he left. While I was there, I asked if I might just say hello and good-bye at the same time. I wished the bishop well in his new assignment.

A few hours later I realized that St. Agatha's parish and I were losing a good friend, but as I said to the bishop, "This is life, so let's go and do the best for God's glory and our commitment."

After all the departures of my friends, I recalled that I had received a call from the publisher who suggested that I write a book about the man who fell in love with his country and send a message to the still young nation.

Part of that message I am able to send is to my students at the university. I love to be in the classroom, to teach and to share my knowledge with young Americans who will be the future leaders of this wonderful country. But sometimes, my second home, the university, makes me worry. I have observed that, for the past five or six years, the students have not been doing as well as they had before. They have been missing more classes and not preparing for classes as they should.

A few weeks before the end of the semester, I confronted the class. I told them that they were damaging themselves by missing classes and coming unprepared. I also told them that these behaviors were especially injurious in foreign languages and sciences. It is necessary to be present in every class in order to build the knowledge in their subject. Learning a foreign language is a gradual process and becomes very rewarding.

The next time we met, one of the students asked me if I had been mad the day I lectured them about attendance. I replied that I wasn't mad, just upset.

"When you miss class, you waste time and money," I said.

I always try to understand the problems of young people, but they have so many excuses. For example, they complain about fighting with their boyfriends or girlfriends as an excuse for not being prepared, or that they cannot sleep or simply cannot study. I feel that their first obligation is to study and not to be wrapped up in their romantic lives. As I continued to talk with them, I said that it is important to be disciplined in order to make a valuable contribution to our society and that their boyfriends or girlfriends should understand that it is important for them to finish their education.

One day when everyone was there in class, I asked them to raise their hand if they were working somewhere, as well as going to school. Most of the hands went up. However, there were times when I had tried to call some of them at work only to learn that they had been fired months before. Their previous employers didn't know how to reach them and didn't care. I think that many of the younger people do not show responsibility for themselves.

I remember that in my youth I had to clean rest rooms in order to afford to attend high school, and I had no place to sleep. Study was very important to me. Also, when I was a full time assistant pastor at a large parish and the pastor was too old to even make sick calls, it was left up to me to visit the sick and elderly. Even if I am pastor, I still do much of the work around the church and rectory. These are duties, and I feel responsible for them. I hope that today's young people will begin to see that they must follow through with their studies.

Even though I sometimes complain about the young people, I realized how attached I had become to my students, even to those who did not attend regularly or study as they should have. When the final test was over, I told them emotionally that I would probably never see them again.

"I truly advise you to study hard. Don't miss classes, and learn self discipline. If you don't learn now, after you have graduated and you get a job working for a large company somewhere, you may not do well or you may even get fired because you were not able to apply yourself," I said.

Then I wished them good luck for the future and told them that I would always be their friend.

What a surprise I had when the class then presented me with an engraved letter opener. One of the more unpleasant students asked me for forgiveness because she had neglected her studies.

I then left the class to go back to the rectory for a good rest and prayers. Above all I was happy that the students had seemed to listen and seemed to want to follow my advice.

The realities of every day direct me in the routine of everyday obligations. Sometimes it is very difficult for me to see the positive aspects of everyday life. Daily mass is a good start for getting into this good routine. I meet people at the office who are usually pleasant, and I feel good when the conversation is friendly. Often I must prepare them for a marriage or a baptism which requires a review of Church doctrine. It is a good opportunity to help the young people renew their own faith.

Other routine items are the mail that comes to the rectory. I find that most of it is junk mail. It is easy to pick out what is important, and I throw the rest in the wastebasket. So much of the junk mail is advertisements that try to sell something to the church. Besides the items that are for sale, there are spaghetti dinners, flea markets, and other ways to get people to spend their money. It is not necessary that I put these announcements in the church bulletin because people do not need to be tempted in these ways.

Once a month I collect all the junk mail in a large plastic bag and throw it in the dumpster. I feel bad that so many companies waste all that paper. Of course, I understand the need for advertising, but it presents many people with the problem of getting rid of their junk paper.

Besides, when the parish needs something, I shop locally. I feel loyal to the local businesses. One of those businessmen is Greg Thomas, an electrician who helps the parish and is usually capable of settling any electrical problems that we may have. He comes on time and is always anxious to help when he can. Another local man who is helpful is Ricardo Unero, a plumber. He was able to repair the water pipes in the church and the other buildings. I really appreciate that he is a polite, hardworking man.

Since I don't live in the safest neighborhood, people often look in on me to see that I am safe. Sometimes Jim Robak, a policeman, stops by to say hello. Because we share a Slavic background, we have a great deal to talk about, and I enjoy having him stop whenever he can. He sometimes gives me instructions on how to handle difficult situations of a criminal nature, should they arise. He told me that I should defend myself if such a situation arose.

"The war is over; now I am a priest as well as a soldier. But I don't think that having a gun means that I should use it to kill someone," I remarked.

As I drank tea with my policeman friend, I wished him well. We both have our own duties. I have a special place in my heart for the police because they try to protect and keep people safe. I pray that God will protect them.

Small things make me happy. When we think we are forgotten, something nice happens to remind us of our good fortune. God rewards us for trying our best.

As I thought about this, the doorbell rang. It was my detective friend, Phillip Goodman. He was smiling broadly because he had become a grandfather. He stopped to share the good news that his daughter had had a baby.

"Remember when my daughter used to help at the rectory, registering offering envelopes?" he asked.

"I remember her," I said. "She always used to be late and always had some excuse not to come to work. And she apologized for her mistakes. But, I told you that she would grow up and lead a good life."

"She became a nurse and moved to Florida, where she got married," Phillip replied.

"That is very good news."

"In a few days, she will come home with the baby. Could you baptize her?" Phillip asked.

"Of course. I will be happy to baptize your new granddaughter, but there will have to be some preparation first," I said.

Phillip remarked, "I still wonder about this generation."

"It's our fault; we spoil them," I retorted.

As I said this, I remembered my own childhood; some of the children were good students even though they were poor. "I remember how happy they were when they received a Christmas gift, how much they appreciated it. Small things made them happy. Today, children will eventually learn how fortunate they are to have devoted parents like you," I told Phillip.

I admire the kindness and compassion with which he raised his six children. I have always been comfortable with this friend. This balances some of the unpleasantness in my life.

After our visit Phillip was going shopping for Christmas gifts. As he left, I shouted, "Don't spend too much; you'll spoil them more." I am sure that he didn't listen to me.

After Phillip left, I went to deliver two books of my poetry to Sister Michael Francis, who is now retired. I learned that she has pneumonia and arthritis. She is old and just celebrated sixty years in the religious life, but she was not able to attend her own celebration. I admire this nun. She is a scholar and professor of English literature. She has a wonderful sense of humor and a strong personality. She is committed to this life.

I used to discuss my books with her. She gave me input and helped me edit and revise the books before they were sent to the publisher. Through Sister Michael Francis I see the presence of God. God's kindness is somehow reflected through this elderly nun. I worry about her because she is ill and not so active. I know what this means to a person who loves to read. I pray that God will protect her and give her strength and many more good years of life.

As I approached the mother house of the sisters, I knew that I would not be able to see Sister Michael Francis, but I had hoped to see the mother superior who was once president of the college where I had taught earlier in my career. Unfortunately, Mother Superior was very busy, but we were able to speak for a few minutes. It had been seventeen years since I last saw her.

How good it is to see our friends after so many years, to know that they are all right and that we are still friends. We both understand that our commitments do not allow us to see each other often.

Later while I sat and reflected on some of these events, I looked up and saw my friend, Major Don Algoode, the R.O.T.C. commander. He had stopped by to visit with me. He gave a friendly salute and we shook hands.

While we were standing there, the commander mentioned that chaplains, like other officers, were to have their uniforms in good shape, clean and neat, and have their hair cut short. I laughed and promised that for the military exercise, the military ball and award ceremony for cadets, I would be in uniform and would also take care to have my hair cut.

After we chatted for a bit, the commander presented me with a schedule for all the military activities which were to take place that month.

After the commander left, I looked at some of my uniforms and decided that the helmet and belt looked as if it had been used in the Second World War, so I went to the Virginia Military Supply Store. The owner, John Frank, replaced all the old stuff for me except the helmet. He said that he didn't have one in the store. However, there was a reserve army staff sergeant also in the store getting some items. He overheard the conversation and approached me and said, "Chaplain, I have three helmets at home. Give me your address and I will send you one of them."

I gave the sergeant my address and thanked him for his kindness. Then I asked John how much I needed to pay for exchanging the military supplies I had brought to the store. I was so surprised when he said, "Chaplain, it is a privilege to help you as you help the United States Army. So we are even."

I thought to myself, "How can I ever be sad, lonely or depressed when people are so nice to me?" For his good and generous heart, I offered to say a mass for John's parents and also for his good health.

Another part of my duties is that I visit a funeral home and say prayers for members who have died. Recently I went to the funeral home and said prayers for a friend who was Catholic, but some of the members of his family were not. These members were in awe that a priest would come to say prayers and were happy and grateful for this show of respect by a Catholic priest.

Later on at the rectory, I received a phone call from the funeral director who asked me if I would bury an older lady who had once belonged to St. Agatha's but had not been a member for many years.

Listening to the story that the director told, I was touched by the situation of the lady, lonely and old, and that Diane Kluska, her niece, had come from California to bury her aunt. She was not sure if I would bury her aunt since she had not been a parishioner for a long time. I told Diane that I would give her the same service I would anyone else. Diane was so pleased that I would do this for her aunt.

It is important to be, at the same time, a priest who deals with Almighty God and keeps contact with Him through all the services and prayers, but also the same person needs to be also sensitive about the beautiful nature in the the world created by God.

A clear sky on the days of work for farmers, or for pilots to fly, are really miracles to look at and to admire. The depth of the oceans, rivers, and lakes and all the life that is in these waters affirm the beauty of the mind of Almighty God. On the earth where we step every day, I see miracles that God performs for us. Do we really take all of these creations for granted? I am sure that each of us does. How generous nature is to us.

Of all of nature's gifts, my favorite are flowers, all sorts of flowers—yellow, white, pink, tulips, roses, petunias, geraniums, and many others—that on this earth create a beautiful carpet. The flowers do not need too much care or knowledge of how to plant them; just pull out the weeds which surround them, and the sun and rain will do the rest. Just looking at them and smelling their sweet aroma makes me happy.

Even though I enjoy looking at these lovely creations, it is also a joy to have others appreciate them. Not long ago the parish received a Beautification Watch Award from the city of Richton, along with a letter thanking the parish for taking such good care of the landscaping and keeping the church property clean. Perhaps this is a small token from the city, but it also shows that, besides God who created nature, there are also earthly authorities who protect and defend nature as well.

Also on the positive outlook on life, I often say that a very strong element in one's religious life, spiritual life, pastoral ministry, or administration is to know he has friends to share friendship.

I have always said that friends never lead priests or other religious people toward evil, but are great assets in their lives. These friends are signs of God's blessing. They are messengers from God, while the priests, as mediators between God and people, perform their duties, fulfill their obligations and, of course, help Christ save people from condemnation, from Hell, and to direct them to eternal happiness, which is the final destiny of human creatures. They are assigned by the Creator to be co-inheritors, brothers of Christ, instruments of proclaiming the Gospel to the world, to all people who are born not to be condemned, as Jesus said, but to be saved. Once they go through this turmoil on earth, go through suffering, perhaps even rejection, sickness and other uncomfortable conditions, the final destiny is eternal happiness in Heaven.

I realize that, besides the loving care of God and His Divine Providence, He provides just people that He called to His ministry as instruments or channels of grace and happiness. The second place is making friends a good asset in our lives. I realize that. How could someone do his best with obligations to administer the sacraments and take care of the parish property without the help of these just people? In spite of ordination and a good education in the priesthood, the best priest could have difficulties if he wanted to do it his way all the time. So, it is not only in the parish council or diocesan priests' councils, but also on the level of parish friends, where there are real treasures and the best assets in that beautiful vocation for giving glory to God and salvation of others.

Good friends do not let the priest become depressed in the moments of difficulties; they cheer him up and give him a hand when he is in need of assistance. They laugh with him. They cry with him; they celebrate any occasion, and above all they pray with him. I realize that, through their activities, their kindness, and their generosity, God Almighty is revealed.

There are some moments in the life of a priest, sometimes critical, that after some very pious prayers he needs assurance from someone, from some place, when his superior is not available. I realize that, at my beginning at St. Agatha's, all the hardships, all the difficulties of a new pastor, turned to blessings from God. I am grateful for help, assistance, prayers, support and, perhaps, even love and understanding of friends, whom I realize God sent for this pastoral mission. More and more I have come to understand that counting all the graces means summarizing the benefits I receive from these friends and from their strong support and encouragement.

For spiritual need, confession is very important in the life of any priest. His heart needs guidance from the same people that were ordained like he was. One of the most powerful privileges for a priest is to say mass every day and to believe, as I do, that *it is more important to us than anything else.* I still continue with dignity and respect saying mass every day and weekend masses as I did for that very first mass I said in my life.

I am tired after all these duties. Every day, prayers in the morning, during the day, and especially in the evening are really uplifting. Often after evening prayers, I feel like going to sleep and that I am ready to give up my body and my soul to Almighty God, my Creator. Prayer strengthens and makes an excellent communication between creature and the great Creator of all creatures.

Sometimes it is necessary to take care of personal matters. One of those is seeing that my car is in good shape. I need that automobile to take me not only to the hospital for sick calls, but also for shopping, going to the university, and for recreation.

When I found out that one of the headlights was out and the mileage on the car showed over sixty thousand miles, I knew that it was time for a check up. I usually do this twice a year. I really was forced to have the headlight fixed. The dealer is located far away, and the repair work there is expensive. This is what a friend told me, and he advised me to take it elsewhere for repairs because it would be less costly.

I finally went to the BP Pro-Care Center where they do this kind of work and was really amazed with Mark Downey, the manager of the place. He was very helpful and kind. While I waited, Mark came to tell me that the radiator fluid smelled rancid. It could cause corrosion in the hoses, so it would need to be flushed and new fluid put in. A few other little items needed to be taken care of, so I told him to get everything fixed.

I continued to wait for this job to get finished. As I did so, I observed people coming and going. One man who came in looked like a member of some sort of organization; he was wearing dark glasses, was not shaved and spoke with a slight foreign accent.

He looked at me and asked me if they were taking good care of me. He called me *preacher*. I responded that I was very satisfied with the service. The man ran his finger across his throat to show what would happen if he was not satisfied with the service. I wondered what was wrong with this man. When Mark came into the waiting room, this man demanded a refund because he was not happy with the repairs made to his car. After he left, Mark told me that the man was not telling the truth, but he gave him a refund because he felt that he did not want a customer who was unhappy.

When I returned home, there was a telephone call from Josephine Fillati, a lonely elderly lady with an Italian background. She cannot come to church and asked to see me so that she could go to confession and receive Holy Communion. I went to the church and picked up the Blessed Sacrament; I really wanted to go to her home since I believe that these older ones are lonely because most of their relatives live far away in Italy or Poland and they have no one close to talk with.

I decided to repay the kindness that Mark had shown by taking a little blooming African violet that I had sitting on the television set. I told myself that this little flower would no doubt make the little lonely lady happy and that there is someone who cares about her. I was right. After confession and Holy Communion, I opened the plastic bag which held the flower and put it on the table for Josephine.

She shouted, "Is this for me?"

"Yes, it is to cheer you up and let you know that there is someone who cares," I replied.

She started to cry and said, "I did not expect that, Reverend."

I then accepted her treat of homemade coffee, which was delicious. It reminded me of my youth when I drank such coffee in Eastern Europe. Even though my doctor had told me that I shouldn't drink coffee, I just did not want to ignore how this little old lady wanted to treat her pastor.

What was amazing about this ninety year old lady was how she recalled, with details, the time when she came to this beautiful country from Italy. She told me how hard she had to work and how good her husband was. Unfortunately, he passed away several years ago. She also had been lucky to have worked for Firestone Tire and Rubber Company and that she made good money which she shared with her relatives living in Italy.

Josephine Fillati told me that, in a vision one day, her mother, father and other members of her family had suddenly appeared to her. She said that they walked from the entrance of the house straight through the living room and dining room without paying any attention to her. She was not sure if it was a vision or a dream, but she decided to pray for them and asked me to say a few masses for them, too. I agreed and told her that I was sure that they would be happy in Heaven and that she praised God in their memory.

From time to time, I recall advice from my friends that I should count the graces in my life. I like to meditate from time to time on the joy in my life.

It took many years for the president of the parish council and me to complete the projects needed to keep the church property in good shape. St. Agatha's parish has three buildings which were built many years ago. Because of the age—the church built almost seventy-five years ago, the parish house and rectory over thirty years ago—it took a lot of hard work and mental stress to get the property looking like it does. For several years the parish president, Angelina, worried as much as I about the expenses connected with the repairing, remodeling, restoring, and fixing of the church property. The time finally arrived when all of this work paid off. Almost all the projects were complete. Most of the credit for their completion belongs to Angelina. She was the overseer of the electricians and carpenters, and she even did much of the work herself. She and I both wanted her to see to the finishing of the painting and cleaning because of the way she completes the work.

I lit a candle for her and her good intentions. Even though she is now retired, she still works part-time at a local bank. Although she is busy, she is always ready and willing to help others in any way she can, and still she had her mind on her mother, Stephanie, a lovely lady who is in a rest home near Richton.

How could a pastoral ministry be successful without such a nice parish council president as Angelina? I am positive that God will reward her for her hard work, her commitment, and for her help, and I know that I, too, appreciate all that she has done.

What a joyful moment for me because all of the projects were completed about ten days before Christmas and there was a meeting of the local bishops and priests.

At the meeting one priest approached me and said, "Michael, I passed St. Agatha's Church, and the whole property looks so clean and neat. What is going on at your place? We know that this parish was never big and never rich and was built by Polish immigrants, but it looks so well kept and not like it has in the past."

"Father Benny, the parish has good people, good spirit, and good heritage," I replied.

Father Benny looked at me and said, "I am sure they have a good janitor and maintenance director."

I just pointed my finger at myself and laughingly said, "Thank you for the recognition."

Also, joy came to me when I was waiting for my friend because we were going to pick up Christmas trees. The doorbell rang, and I thought it was my friend. But, when I opened the door and looked out, there was no one there. There was no car, so I took a cane, as it was dark outside, and walked around the rectory. I found no one. As I walked back to the rectory, I noticed that a big package was left in the milk box. I took it inside, opened it, and found a smaller package inside which contained the graduation ring I had from a university in Hopeland. I had sent it for repairs as the center stone had broken. I had dropped the ring on a concrete floor when I was taking it off my hand to lay on the kitchen counter. The ring had either been fixed or replaced because it looked like new. I did not know that the Artcraft Company in Texas had a lifetime warranty on its rings. This brought joy and happiness to know that business people care about their customers and do what is right. May God bless the good people who cheer us up when we are overworked or depressed. Both the work of the parish council and the master's degree ring being repaired made for great joy just before the Christmas season.

When I am able to take any time off, I like to walk around Chapelgate Mall. It had been some time since I had wandered around the mall. It was good to just relax, and as I walked, I smiled at the people who were also walking and looking in the many store windows.

This time there was a boat show in the mall, so I stopped and looked at all the beautiful boats. While I looked, I remembered the beautiful lake of Mazury. I had a small, well-used boat, and I traveled from village to village where I taught religion in the schools. In the villages there were very pleasant children and families where, to me, it felt like a second home. I spent many happy hours in that lake area. Seeing all the boats in the mall reminded me of how life passes by so fast. How great God is to allow me to land in this country.

After looking at all the boats, I continued down the mall until I came to the Fieldcrest Company. Suddenly, I heard a voice from the past say, "How are you?"

I recognized Marge Markey, a saleslady there. I said to her, "Do you really want to know how I am? Why?"

I said that I felt funny now in this place where the salespeople used to be more friendly. I asked Marge where these people were and what had happened to them.

"Well," Marge said, "that's the changing times."

She then told me that in her congregation the people kicked their minister out because he ruined the church financially. The congregation dropped in membership from two hundred to only fifty members.

I responded, "Listen, Marge, in my experience when I listen to some ministers' and rabbis' stories, it seems that people expect too much from their religious leaders today. What did he do wrong?"

"He was for himself and did not organize social activities. Those societies kept us together, so when we did not have them, the people went someplace where they could get this kind of ministry."

"Marge," I remarked, "believe me, the social activities are not the most important events of the church. Aren't we priests, ministers and rabbis called to be spiritual leaders—to lead the congregation in prayers, devotions, reflections for praising God and helping people to be reconciled with God and love Him and love our neighbors?

"Marge," I continued, "I would not like the smell of sausage or stuffed cabbage in my church. I like to see people praying, and I like to listen to them singing and see them going home somehow renewed and ready to face all of life, whatever it brings."

Marge looked at me and said that she liked my ideas and that it was nice to chat with me, but that she now had to continue with her work. She also agreed that times were changing and with the changes come different people. As we parted, we promised to pray for each other, and then we said good-bye.

Before I left Marge's department, one of my parishioners, Joe Kontent, stopped, smiled and greeted me. As he stood there, the scar from his recent surgery was visible at the top of his open shirt.

"Isn't God great? Medicine helped you and so many people to survive difficulties and sickness, so some should be grateful to God," Joe said.

"Yes, I have seen this hundreds and hundreds of times in my life," I agreed. "Praise be to God for that."

Marge just looked at us.

"See, Joe's presence shows you a successful pastoral ministry." I told Joe jokingly that we should take up a collection after our discussion.

I left the smiling Joe and Marge knowing that the chat had been good for both of them.

This encounter with Marge made me think about others who are in the same situation as I am. My experience with my brother priests, partners in the pastoral ministry, is a very positive one. Visiting other parishes is rare because I am so busy at my own place with services, devotions or activities. Sometimes I am unable even to attend meetings with other priests. Still, I feel spiritually united with them. It is amazing that at important meetings I meet some priests that I haven't seen for fifteen or twenty years because the diocese of Hopeland is a very large one. Still the relationships are cordial as we share the same problems of everyday life and have the same willingness to do the best for our parishes.

I am always happy when I am able to attend the meetings with the bishops and other priests. Often they are once a month, and the atmosphere is pleasant and friendly. The bishops show great leadership, and the priests show concern for their parishes and the Church in general. After I leave these meetings, I am happy to be a part of the diocese where I am privileged to be a pastor. For this I am grateful to God and to my past and present superiors.

Another part of my life involves being a R.O.T.C. chaplain, and in that capacity I, in full dress uniform, took part in the *dining-in* for cadets and officers from five universities. Just before I was to deliver the benediction, I made some remarks.

"Dear friends, before we hear the benediction, I would like you to hear the advice of a presiding general, Vincent Oldi, who said that sometimes we must have fun in our leadership and not always be serious. At the time, there were strong feelings about the war in the Persian Gulf. I am still amazed about General Schwarzkopf when Betty Wellman, on her TV program, showed his quarters in the Gulf. The general happily showed Betty the picture of his family. I felt that there must be a kind of loving heart behind the uniform of that general. But I also noticed something else in the general's quarters. I noticed that the general had teddy bears, twelve of them. I thought, if the general likes teddy bears, then we must have something in common. Of course, I had only six teddy bears. Now I will not hide my teddy bears, which are all over my home, when my bishop or other priests visit me. I feel proud to have them."

Then I took a little teddy bear from a sandwich bag, and I asked Mr. Donald Wise, who was in charge of this dining-in to approach the podium.

"For the outstanding evening you have organized, I wish to present you with this teddy bear. It symbolizes a good human heart in these difficult times," I told him.

All of the cadets and officers laughed as Mr. Wise took the teddy bear from me.

"Thank you," he said. "I will put this bear on the shelf with my Cabbage Patch dolls."

When the ceremony was over and after wishing everyone success in their studies and their lives, I went home. I hope that they, besides becoming good soldiers, will also have fun and not always be so serious.

Not only do I enjoy the company of the military men, but I like to be with my clergy friends as well. I especially remember a young monsignor who later became our bishop and how he smiled so much and was not always serious either. This young monsignor, Bernard O'Neill, also interceded for me with Bishop Christopher when I wanted to continue my graduate studies in Ottawa. When my book, *The Priest Who Came to America*, was published, the bishop sent me a wonderful letter and encouraged me to continue with my writing.

So, when my second book was printed, I invited the bishop to have lunch with me at a Slavic restaurant. It was a happy occasion, and we spent hours talking and reminiscing about the past twenty-eight years. I was sad to say good-bye to my friend.

Now as I sit here thinking of the past, I remember a strange situation on my seventeenth anniversary at St. Agatha's Parish. An elderly woman came to talk to me after mass. She shook my hand and looked at me seriously.

"You know, Father Michael," she said, "it will be exactly seventeen years on July 17th that you arrived at this parish as pastor. Can you imagine that it was on a Wednesday that year, too? So now, you little Polish priest, tell me, how do you like this parish? How much have you changed since the time you came here? I remember you when you first came, wearing blue pants and brown shoes. You even rode a motorcycle. You didn't look like you meant business like your predecessor. He was a good administrator, and his pockets were lined with money."

I don't know why she was so merciless, but I still like her. I do remember that I had been wearing gray shoes and I tried to hide them with my cossack.

She carried on, but it was time for me to go to the rectory for a little rest before the next mass.

I looked at her and said, "I feel like choking you. Why don't you shut up? Why bring up the unpleasant when there are so many good things that have happened in those seventeen years, thanks to God and His people?"

The old lady answered me, "Since you told me to shut up, you are my boy. I like you. You're an American now, and you speak

American!" And then she hugged me. I felt really good, and I walked to the rectory smiling to myself.

Even as I reflect on the positive side of the ministry, I often think that we are much under the influence of sensational news media. Perhaps there is even a tendency to investigate the negative side of the imperfect human beings. The media questions the people and looks for the bad side of their lives. Where do they go? With whom do they associate? And, of course, always looking for the rumors and gossip about people. And we, as humans, also read and watch all of this. Usually, if we like the person the media mentions, we sympathize with his or her troubles and forgive whatever he or she has done; if we don't like the individual, we condemn him or her, which is wrong. Who could really know what is in the human heart? Only God!

Who are we to condemn the other sinners if we are also sinners? We should turn to our Lord more than to people whom we really don't trust, and we should ask God for forgiveness. We try again and again to find some patterns of *holiness* and *perfection*, mostly by imitating the kindness and compassion of Jesus and by looking for a good model of holy people who also suffer, achieve, perhaps even fail sometimes, but who don't give up.

Once, in my parish, I had a conversation with a strange man who asked if he could have a private talk with me at the rectory. He said his name was John Thomas. He acted happy, but I noticed in his face suffering which may have lasted for some time. He was sentenced, he said, to many years in jail for his stupidity when he was young.

"Father Michael," he said, "I really deserved what I got, but I should have stayed in the jail longer. That really changed my life. So, I have come to ask you to forgive me. I want to convert to God. First with many thanks that it happened in my life, but also I pray that my relatives and friends will accept me back. Some of them are alive, but I wonder if they will still like me and accept me."

"Don't count on support only from the people," I told him. "They may accept you back but there is one man, our Savior, who also died for us, and He said, 'I did not come to destroy the world or to condemn, but to save.' I am positive He touches you directly, otherwise you would not have come to the priest in the church, but perhaps you would have gone to a tavern to celebrate your return to freedom. Again I repeat what Jesus said to the sinners, 'Please go in peace and sin no more.' *Your* sins, after repentance and a change of your lifestyle, of course, and after confession, God will forgive you."

John, with tears in his eyes, left the rectory. As he left, I saw a different expression on his face. I promised to say a prayer for him and for his health and blessing. So, the people joined me in saying prayers for John at the masses during that weekend.

I sometimes wonder why people seem to hunger for condemnation. It looks as if they wish to have something bad happen to someone. Somehow it is very painful for me, and always will be, to read articles or to hear from the television about so many scandals, lack of faithfulness, murderers, destruction of young innocent lives, drug abuse, and child abuse, but I know through my experiences that there are many good people around us.

What about the simple grandma who comes to St. Agatha's. She is a little loud with her voice and makes more noise with her cane; she wears an old babushka with holes in it on her head. She noisily approaches the confessional or to receive Holy Communion, but I see a greatness in this old-fashioned Polish-American *babchi* (grandma). There is holiness, piety, and a great image of faithful Polish-American immigrants who worked very hard to achieve all she possesses besides her cane and babushka; she is very dear to her children and to her grandchildren.

I like to say mass in Polish for those elderly immigrants. I was once asked why I did not cancel this mass or have it in English. I responded simply, "I am not going to betray my senior parishioners who built two churches and have supported it with their kindness and generosity for over eighty years. That is a long time for them to put their hearts and souls into it, and it is a spiritual treasure that is located here at St. Agatha's Church."

There was a very good outcome in the church after the Second Vatican Council; women were more welcome to take part in the pastoral ministry, reading from the pulpit on various occasions, especially the Holy Week Triduum celebration. I welcomed this and realized how beautifully they read.

Monica Zdolny is over seventy years old. She not only is in charge of religious instructions for children, but also for the past fifteen years has made progress in her education in the knowledge of the doctrines of the Church, for which she has received awards and certificates.

Mary Kurant, who belongs to the ladies auxiliary of the veterans, along with her family came to our parish to share her kindness and generosity.

Each day I thank God for these kind and wonderful people who have and continue to help our parish.

Above all I count the many graces that have come to this parish, and I strongly believe that Divine Providence will not abandon the immigrants who built and organized the parish and their children who continue to keep the place neat and holy.

I still remember long ago that, as a young priest just after my ordination, I was called at midnight by a brother-custodian of the parish where I was a guest. This brother looked like old St. Francis. He carried a bunch of old-fashioned keys on his belt, and he had long red hair and a beard. I had met him at a convalescent home where he had been recuperating from an illness and we had chatted there. After the mass, Brother Anthony stopped at the sacristy and said, "Would you like to catch a big fish with me sometime?"

"You see," he continued, "in our town, many people look for a priest with compassion, not only to listen to confessions but also to talk with them outside the confessional."

"Yes, I would like to go fishing any time; just tell me when, and I'll be there on time," I replied.

At two o'clock in the morning, a nun from that same convalescent home knocked on my door and said that Brother Anthony called for me.

"Sorry, Father," she said, "but at this time you know it is an emergency. He has a big fish for you. Get up; go to the side door of the church by the altar of St. Francis. It is open, and Brother will meet you there."

I, laughing and talking a little, said to myself, "What kind of fish is this that awakens me at two o'clock in the morning?"

Although I was tired and not really in good health, I know I would do anything for the salvation of others. I got up, washed my face, put on my cossack and, with a cane in one hand and a rosary in the other, went straight to the church. The brother was waiting for me, and there in the corner of the church by the side altar of St. Francis, stood a husky, pleasant and nervous man. He requested that we talk outside the confessional. He introduced himself as a colonel of the secret communist police who was vacationing in our town.

He said that he was disturbed by his conscience since in his district of Krakow he was in charge of arresting and imprisoning clergy. Of course, he did investigate and falsify evidence and turn them over to the communist judges. He even sent some of them to labor concentration camps, perhaps even to Siberia, and some were even executed.

I couldn't believe what I was hearing. Could it be a dream, or was it reality? The big fish, a secret communist police colonel, seemed to me worse than the devil at that moment, but I looked up at the altar. From the ceiling hung an eternal vigil light which showed the presence of the one great Son of God, and I almost screamed, "God help me! Perhaps I am too young to deal with such a difficult situation."

But, then I remembered what the bishop said at my ordination. "When you perform any of your priestly duties, you will be just fine because the grace of God and my prayer will be with you always." I finished the meeting with my priestly duty; I did what I had to do as a priest.

When I came to the United States, still a very young priest, I set my goals to study and to adjust to this new country. Of course, I was away from politics, but I wanted to commit myself to be the best as a priest and as a citizen in my newly adopted country. But, from time to time, someone would question me about my experiences during the German occupation and of my participation in defending or protecting my fatherland with thousands and thousands of other comrades, young soldiers and officers.

The newspaper *Press* in Hopeland, Ohio, interviewed me when I was an assistant pastor at St. Martha's in the southern part of

Hopeland. The title of the interview with my picture in my biretta was a little unpleasant as it was made solely for sensation. The title was "Polish Priest with Memories of the Red Army." I had never been in the Red Army; it was the Polish Army organized from Polish prisons mostly in the Soviet Union. Some information can be so misleading.

In that article it mentioned that I would write a book about my life's experiences. Years passed by, and I was so busy studying, working in my new parish, receiving my master's degree, teaching in college and later studying for my Ph.D. that I didn't have time to write that book.

From time to time I continued to write poems which I had started when I was fourteen. The climax of my writing was two years after receiving my Ph.D. from the University of Ottawa. I wrote *The Priest Who Came to America*, which is a novel based on true stories of my personal experiences, and it was published by Winston-Derek of Nashville, Tennessee. The book sold quite well at the University of Richton. The local newspaper wrote a nice article about me after the book was published. I was pleased with the title of the article, which was "Learning to Forgive."

The forgiveness was for Germans who occupied Poland and destroyed many lives and our lovely cities. Forgiveness did not come from the heart of the soldier, but from the heart of the priest. I felt that forgiveness.

Encouraged by my friends, I also put together a book of poems. Again a representative from the newspaper where I live interviewed me and wrote an article about my poems; he also interpreted my poems as well.

4

Reaching Out Ministry

This chapter portrays not only a person as a priest who loves his vocation, but also unusual circumstances and situations he encounters as the pastor at St. Agatha's Church. Father Michael, at the same time he is a military chaplain, a teacher at the university, a preacher, novelist, and a poet, is also a cook, yardman, and snow shoveler.

Through historical events, Father Michael's reaching out was significant because of his acquaintances and friends in the diplomatic corps. They often visited him from Washington, D. C., New York and foreign countries and shared political and diplomatic views with him. They received spiritual assistance from him.

As the pastor of St. Agatha's I was very happy about the possibility of also reaching outside the parish. This ministry reaches to groups, as well as to individuals, and extends as far away as New York and Washington, D.C. My contact with diplomats and even with scientists is important in this outreach. Some were researchers or visiting professors at the university where I met them. They attended my church, and we have kept in touch even after they have gone on to other places and other things.

While I think about some of those people who have moved on to other jobs and other places, I remember one hot Thursday evening when I heard the phone ring. It was Jola Sport from Delaware, who was a friend and former parishioner. She came to this country with her husband who was in the exchange program at the University of Richton. I hadn't seen them for almost seven years. They were in town for a week while her husband attended a convention in the Polymer Science Department at the university.

It was early the next Monday morning when I met Jola and her husband and son in a joyful reunion. There were memories and news of the past seven years to catch up on. I congratulated them on their success. They both work for a famous polymer company, and they realize how fortunate that they are to have come from Poland and are now able to enjoy this country and all that it offers.

Their son Misha, a growing thirteen year old, is a straight-A student and is turning into a pleasant young man. Jola's husband talked about other Polish scholars who were attending the convention. He mentioned a professor of polymer science who had sought asylum in the '70s. He returned to Poland and was involved in Solidarity and was arrested, but was released with the collapse of Communism. The new government rewarded him for his commitment to the underground, and he was appointed deputy minister of education for the new Polish government. Now he is the ambassador to Canada.

Jola and her family were busy for the next few days with meetings and dinners. It is amazing how busy people can be. When the convention was over, we said our good-byes and promised to keep in touch.

Afterwards, as I sat there, I thought about my forty years in the priesthood. It was the 29th of June, and I opened the windows of the church and saw two cardinals. I listened to them sing throughout the mass, and I was glad to have my loneliness eased a little.

I announced my anniversary two weeks later and said that I wanted only to celebrate in the church. I did not want a banquet, but would hand out booklets about the anniversary at no charge to the parishioners. I felt that the best gift on my anniversary was a peaceful coexistence between the parishioners and me and that the church was in good shape and beautifully landscaped and cared for.

On Saturday evening after I conducted a mini spiritual renewal, I was surprised when some people from the parish took me to the Polish-American Veterans' Club for a cordial and private dinner. I enjoyed their company and told them that for at least one evening I would not have to peel potatoes. I hadn't wanted anything like this, but was happy that they thought of me.

The next day I said three masses where I stressed that the most important things in my life were the joys and happiness that I experienced in my parish. People were friendly to me and wished me many more happy years at St. Agatha's.

As I look back I am grateful to God and to my friends, that I have been able to survive in what was known as a difficult parish, and that I have been able to enjoy my time here. Part of the success is due to my being able to keep a balance between the parish life and reaching out to students through my teaching and my chaplaincy. Credit also goes to all my parishioners, friends, students, faculty, officers and commanders. To all of them I say thank you.

In some of my reflections, I question what's going on with the Church today. I question myself, my friends, and my brother priests.

Even though the pastoral and administrative duties are usually smoothly fulfilled, there are things which bother me. I know that I don't need too many people to maintain the parish spiritually or materially. The administrative offices in Hopeland, however, have continued to grow over the years. It has become more and more like a business.

This is not an accusation, but a reality. There are specialists who tell parishes what to do. I admire those who are privileged to be bishops, but I wonder how they sleep when they must constantly deal with the pastoral problems. There has been considerable change among the bishops—they are more brotherly and have less tendency to show their power toward their priests in an effort to be with them. At the diocesan level, there are many who work in administration, but they may not know exactly what is going on at the parish level. They may not know that I am not only priest, but cook and professor, janitor and colonel. I open the church, shovel snow, mow the grass, then administer the sacraments and serve as chaplain for the Army R.O.T.C. I still get good instructions from the main office of the diocese telling me how to conduct my parish affairs.

Most of the time it helps, but I don't much care for the local religious newspapers, although they occasionally have nice articles. These papers were inherited from the previous pastor, and since they are local publications, I have kept them, even though the people don't care for them either.

I received a pamphlet concerning continuing education for ministers. There are many interesting topics listed there offered by Catholic colleges and institutions, but there is an unpleasant introduction. It was written by F. John Bingoli. It was disgusting to me. He mentioned Brother Bambino who is on the faculty of a Jesuit university, the Institute of Pastoral Study in Chicago.

Brother Bingoli writes about the situation in the contemporary church: "The old is fading, dying and ending, but there is still a little life in it struggling. The new is not year clear; the 'not yet' is not yet here."

Who is Brother Bambino? From whence comes his authority, and on what experience does he base his statement? He offends millions of faithful Catholics, among whom are many clergy who have worked for decades in the pastoral ministry.

Didn't Jesus say, "I will not leave you orphans?" Did He not promise to send teachers who would tell us what to do? Are we not to remember His words "not to be afraid"?

We should not be afraid of the changing world, but we should continue to cherish tradition. Isn't the Bible the foundation of our faith? And it wasn't written in the nineties. And wasn't the Old Testament, with its prophecies of a Messiah, a worthy preface to the coming of our Lord? The beautiful forecasting of our Lord's coming cannot be overshadowed by the demonstrations and protestations against the tradition of the Church's position on earth. They are undermining the Church's authority.

There they go again forgetting the commitment which is so essential to the continuation of the Church and to its prospering in the future.

The pamphlet describes many courses which are offered, but I wonder if they are teaching what is important to the continuation of the Church's ministry. If the introduction reflects the contents of what is offered, perhaps it should be questioned. On the other hand, if they are offered in the spirit of serving the Archpriest, Christ, and His Institution, perhaps they have value.

I receive many letters and magazines which help priests in their pastoral ministries, but some of them reflect the subtle undermining of the priest's mission. One, *The Priest*, promises to "restore your vision and your ability, help make you a more effective speaker, a smarter manager, and a more inspirational example of Christianity in Action."

I wonder about the experience accumulated over forty years in the priesthood and the excellent training in the seminary and my education at the university and in graduate school.

All things, whether conferences or meetings, have their costs. How can anyone afford to attend meetings or retreats or subscribe to magazines when they live in a small parish that cannot even afford a housekeeper or a janitor?

But, most of all, I believe that there should be mutual prayer to God for a world in which there is no prayer. There is increasing crime on the streets and lack of respect for God and for each other.

If there is a shortage of priests, could it be because we have spoiled our children? Have they grown up without a sense of commitment to their families, communities and churches? They have learned to be selfish and to live without God. Something terrible has happened over the past twenty years in the United States: millions of children have been aborted.

These reflections on our society are not sources of controversy— they are realities and have been realities for many years. It is sad, but there is hope in the possible renewal through Christ. But it will not come about through the expending of resources for profit.

Besides God, there are the people of God. When I meet with my friend the bishop, I sense his gentleness and commitment. I love those meetings where we share ideas. He is brotherly and easy to talk to, and I feel that it is a special gift from God to have a friend such as he.

As much as I want to be open-minded, I pray that God will protect His Church from liberal personalities. I cannot see the Church run by a majority of lay people. Many of my friends agree with me when we discuss this matter.

After a variety of meetings, which are normal for my position, and being able to rest a little, I began to relax and to feel good and began to realize that I no longer felt like *a stranger in a strange land.* In 1994, I will have been in the pastoral ministry at St. Agatha's for more than twenty years. At the beginning of the year I realized how many years had passed at this parish and how I truly love it.

I like to reflect on the two weeks of services connected with Christmas and the New Year, and as I do, I realize that there is a great satisfaction in serving a small ethnic parish.

The joy of Christmas is overshadowed by something that only a priest can understand. I am very concerned about my ministry to aging parishioners. For years I regularly visited them, some for many years, but there also are those whom I visit because they are ill.

The first Friday of the month is the time that I set aside to give spiritual comfort to elderly parishioners and to those who are unable to attend the church. My heart truly suffers because as I visit them I see their suffering, even though they welcome me cordially. We chat and I give them comfort by administering Holy Communion, the center of Catholic religious life. We pray together before I leave, but they are with me all of the time.

I also admire those who care for those who are ill and unable to leave their homes. But sometimes I am confronted with people who neglect those in their care, and especially are neglectful of their spiritual needs.

It is possible that some grandparents have written a will and left their money to those who care for them. When this happens, the caregiver is happy to provide for them, but after a while the situation is not so pleasant. I could never understand why these relatives change so and can hardly wait for the loved one to die.

One woman's daughter expressed herself to me. "My mother died on my birthday, and it was the best gift she could have given me." I was so shocked when she said this.

At another place someone offered me money to light a candle in the church and to pray that his father would die.

"On the contrary, I will pray that he will live. It is terrible what you are asking me to do. Always I will pray for someone to live," I replied.

"But, Father, there is twenty-five dollars in it for you for the funeral," he said.

But I responded, "As long as they are alive, people are worth more than *millions* of dollars."

There is one home where I have difficulty visiting, even though the family knows that I like to visit their sick relative. Often they ignore my knock, and I must go home and call to let them know that I plan to visit. Once when I explained that I would like to bring Holy Communion for their relative, they did not receive me very well. When I finally was able to have someone open the door, the person was still in her nightgown, even though it was noon. I gave the elderly relative the Sacrament. She told me that her son-in-law was unemployed and drank a lot of beer. As I was leaving, I asked the daughter to call me in case of an emergency, which she promised to do.

A few days later, another relative approached me and expressed regret at the way I had been treated while trying to visit her relative. She told me not to feel bad, that this was not a family of practicing Catholics. I thanked her, but asked that she call me if I was needed, and she promised that she would.

After I got home, I sat and thought about the positive side of this strange land in which I found myself. I know that after these experiences it is difficult to see the good, but I know that it is really there and I must always look for it.

I no longer consider myself a stranger. I feel firmly established here. God has given me a feeling of comfort and peace, and the people are friendly for the most part. No matter where I go, even to the bishop's office, I am welcomed.

Even when I go shopping, cashiers and employees in stores often ask me how I am and if they can do something to help me. At the place where I have bought flowers for years, the workers sometimes invite me to have soup for lunch with them. I always enjoy this time because the soup is homemade and the people are friendly.

The clerks used to call me *Father Discount* because I was not always able to afford things even with a discount. But for many years now I have bought my flowers and bushes and paid full price for them, so I no longer have that nickname.

Not far from the church is a couple who runs a little cafe. Maria and her husband are always generous with doughnuts and hot chocolate. We chitchat when I go there to buy their delicious bread.

The place where I also feel at home is at the university. My friends tell me that it is good for me to teach part-time at the university while I am a full-time pastor. A good friend told me that it makes it possible for me to have some sense of being in my life.

I am always excited to start my new classes at the university. My students learn a foreign language, and they also study literature and culture. These are not easy for everyone, but fortunately most of the students are good learners. I have a good relationship with the students, and in spite of my friendliness toward the students, I realize that my loyalty is to knowledge and to the university, so I mean business while I teach.

The semesters pass by quickly, one right after another. Usually, my students only stay one year, but some stay longer as friends. When it is time to say good-bye, I am sad, but when new students arrive, I make new friends.

As I prepare for my classes, I know that teaching exercises the mind. I especially like the advanced classes in literature and culture, which I taught for many years, where students do research and discuss these ideas in classes. They sing and recite poems, but sometimes we share cookies and pizza together, too.

From time to time I recall the good memories of over thirty years ago when I was pastor at St. Andrew's Church in Poland. It was a region where there are over one thousand lakes. I remember how pleasant it was sometimes to get out from the parish and go for a ride in my car. The car was very small, only a two-cylinder, and not very expensive to operate. I derived a great deal of pleasure from driving the car on roads which ran between the beautiful lakes and hills.

Before I left Poland I took a tour driving around Poland with my friend, Father Walter Wielkolud. It was a pleasant time. When I passed by, people greeted me with smiles. There was no problem with parking in small or even big cities because the people did not have many cars in Poland as they did in the United States.

This good feeling, while driving around in my car, was lost to me when I came to this country. When I was an assistant pastor, the car was used a lot for visiting parishioners for so-called *house blessings*, to go to the university for classes, to college to teach, for visitations of sick people, and for saying the rosary at funeral homes. At some places I even served as chauffeur for pastors when they went to play golf or to take the housekeeper shopping.

The car is a blessing from God. It really helps people work more fruitfully. It is also unpleasant having a car. First of all, the car eats gasoline, and maintaining it is expensive. All kinds of repairs are costly. Fortunately, the church authorities realize this and give some allowance for driving for pastoral duties.

Even though this vehicle is a benefit, it causes a great deal of traffic in the bigger cities. Most of the people who drive do not observe the speed laws. Usually those people go at least ten miles over whatever is the speed limit. Another of the difficult things these people do is to ride too close to the back of another car, but the worst thing is that they do not use their turn signals to show in which direction they wish to go.

Most of the people passing by at a high rate of speed have an angry look upon their faces when someone is following the speed limit. They also, in a very ugly way, give the driver *the finger*, which means something terrible. They don't seem to care that they might be offending the other drivers on the road with their ugly gestures.

One time I followed some teenagers who showed their fingers because I had stopped in front of them and they had to stop, too. I asked them, "Why do you have to be so ugly to people who are only driving the correct way?"

The boys were ready to fight, got out of their car, and wanted to attack me. I told them that they might get a surprise if they tried to fight because I am an officer in the army and I know how to defend myself and that I would take off my collar. I asked them, "Do you want to fight?" But they chickened out and left in a hurry.

God needs to be merciful to the drivers in this beautiful country. Sometimes I am so frustrated that I want to scream, "God help us because of the careless drivers on the roads." These terrible drivers cause a lot of stress, headaches, and stomach aches to those of us who have to use the highways for our work and professions, but I believe that one day the authorities will prosecute bad drivers the way they do the drug dealers and other criminals. Perhaps then we will be protected from this harassment.

After all of this thought about drivers and the problems they cause, I relaxed and spent some time with my friends, and we ate homemade bread and drank apple juice. It was good to be able to forget those kinds of problems and enjoy good people.

I am grateful for being cheered by my friends. There has always been someone over the past twenty years who has helped me to stay safely in my neighborhood. I feel comfortable because of the support of people, and I want to stay and to continue my work with them.

To some it may seem like fun, and perhaps it is fun, to be invited to lunches and other functions by the deputy mayor, Angelo Stazio, Mayor Francis Smith, and the city prosecutor, John Justman, but to me they are very good and dear friends. Their companionship is really an extension of the pastoral ministry. And though these times have been limited, they have been very pleasant.

I listened to what these friends experienced working for the city; their struggles, their achievements, and their commitment to their occupations and duties show me how city officials really care about the people who work for them.

The city prosecutor, for example, shared a very dangerous experience with us. A young lady filed a complaint against her boyfriend. The prosecutor went and listened to her, but couldn't believe that, without any reason, her boyfriend mistreated her, scared her and finally beat her up. He had listened with compassion, but decided to check her out on the computer. What he found was shocking, and he called the police, who told him that she was dangerous because she usually carried a big butcher knife. A woman police officer came in and questioned the woman. They found after a search that she was carrying a big knife, so she was arrested for having a concealed weapon.

When he finished telling the story, we decided that we must be living in a sick and selfish society. I felt privileged that the city prosecutor shared this story with me.

I questioned myself, "Who am I to complain when people repay you with ugliness when it appears to be something else?"

Lunch continued, and while we enjoyed the meal, the deputy mayor, from time to time, shared his experiences, and so did I. After a while we promised that we should see each other within the next few weeks to cheer each other up with our daily commitments and duties.

At that time I remembered an experience I'd had with some strange people in the neighborhood. A young man came to the rectory and knocked on the door. I opened it and invited the man inside, and then he asked me for $250. I was shocked and replied, "I don't have that kind of money."

He didn't ask in a nice way, but demanded the money. I explained that, because of the size of the parish, this kind of money was not available, but he continued angrily to demand the money or something of value that he could sell.

Fortunately, the telephone rang at that time. When I answered, I pretended to ask a police lieutenant, who comes by to visit occasionally, to come quickly as I needed help. The young man had stood up, and I saw a shiny object in his hand that I knew to be a knife. However, when he heard my conversation, he opened the door and ran. I certainly was glad to see him leave.

We are able to see again and again that sometimes we need our friends because we need to talk with them about our struggles, especially when we have had events such as these. The friends who work with us, who care about us, who pray for us, and who support us with their encouragement are a great asset in our lives. It is important that we realize it and appreciate it.

Though we always try to do our best, not everything goes according to our wishes from time to time. But, if not for friends, perhaps we would become depressed and unhappy.

I remember the time when Angelina wrote a beautiful poem concerning the time when I came from Europe sixteen years before, and how my beginning was difficult, but I did not give up. I like to read this poem from time to time, and I smile because I know that it was written by a friend who has done tremendous work for the parish, not only good work on parish finances, but also spiritually by being the president of the parish council for several years. There is no doubt that she deserves special recognition for her time, compassion, understanding, hard work, and good advice to help me keep the parish in good condition. She does this from the goodness of her heart and wants no special recognition, but thanks to her and to all the council members and the good people, the parish is in good shape.

Only God knows how Angelina and others have cheered me up, helped me, and prayed for me to survive the difficult beginning I had to endure when I came here.

There are many ways to discourage people, but someone should be proud to encourage, help, and support a priest in his pastoral ministry for his flock.

"It is not always easy for pastor," said Angelina to a group of supporters and even to other priests and friends of mine. But I do realize that in my forty years of priesthood there is a lot of joy and a positive side, and sometimes a serious and difficult side to spiritual leadership. However, I also experience a feeling of joy to be a worker of Christ in His vineyard.

The University of Richton is my second home. As I think about this great privilege of teaching, I, on my knees, thank God that He and my superiors have allowed me to be involved in this beautiful country's intellectual life, that of being connected with teaching.

After long study toward a doctorate, I really matured in knowledge of my subject and not only grew up, but started to love it and to truly enjoy it.

Someone once asked me, "Why do you do it?" I very simply like to tell everyone who asks that the education I gained in my life makes my faith stronger, more appreciative for the priesthood and my commitment toward the Church. So, my part-time teaching helps me to be organized with my intellect and, perhaps, even to be dressed neater for meeting people, not the same way as when I cut the grass or shovel snow.

I really enjoy seeing the crowd at the university, the many students and professors, and I feel fortunate that the president of the university became a close friend who cherished my ideas and activities and respected me not only as a teacher, but also as a man who devoted his life to God. But the happiest times for me at the university are with my group of personal contacts among the students. I believe that the young people, who are full of new ideas, hopes, and their struggles to achieve the goals in their lives, have a tremendous influence on me. Even though I am much older than my students, I feel that I am accepted among them.

I have never thought that my role as a professor was like babysitting. My first worries and my first task is to share knowledge with the students, to encourage them to memorize the vocabularies, and then to translate, decline, conjugate, and many other grammatical exercises. Conversation in a foreign language with Americans makes me feel good. Generally speaking, I do not give bad grades if the students make an effort to learn. Americans are smart, but sometimes they take things for granted. Some of them are lazy and do not expect to work for their grades.

Of course, it is important to like, perhaps even to love, the profession of teaching, but I am grateful to God for my good feeling towards students whom I really want to help. I am not pushy to make friends or to have followers, but I just want them to know that I will help them if they need it.

There are some students who feel the need to talk to me privately. I know some of them have no one else to talk to. Some are away from home, fight with their boyfriends or girlfriends, are short of cash, become fatigued after getting ready for quizzes and tests, and need to be able to talk with someone about these problems, so they call me or stop by the rectory. I like them to do so because this kind of relationship reminds me of the time when I studied at the seminary and also at the universities.

One example of someone who needed to talk with me happened not long ago. I received a telephone call from one of the students who was going through a divorce from her husband. When I listened to the message from her, I could not ignore Antoinette Singali's call. I returned her call and listened to this very unpleasant conversation. As she cried, Antoinette Singali said, "I have to talk with you, my professor Father Michael, because I am depressed and can't stand any longer to go through all the circumstances connected with this divorce. Please, be patient with me; I know that I have neglected your class. My husband's visitation with the children makes the situation worse. He brings money for the children that I cannot offer them, since I only work part-time, and that spoils them. He is trying to gain their hearts even though he left them after years of marriage."

I promised to pray for her and to listen to her anytime that she needed to call. But, in my heart, I just pray that God will help her and her children to survive this difficult time in their lives. I am sure that she is doing the right thing by getting more education, for in the future, as a single parent, she has to look for a better job to support her family.

Fortunately, in America, I have learned to be open-minded toward different nationalities, colors of skin, and religions. The University of Richton is predominantly made up of Protestants. I know it is amazing that, as a Roman Catholic priest, I have so many friends among these Protestants. As I used to say, "We have many good things in common. First of all, we study together, and the most important thing we have in common in our lives is Jesus."

However, I do not mix my pastoral ministry with my teaching because of the respect I have for freedoms of religion. I am proud that I am allowed to teach at a state university and that nobody objects when I wear the collar of a priest.

Even though I enjoy my teaching, I also look forward to the vacation time. One of the pleasant experiences that touched my heart very deeply was when a captain from the Military Science Department was promoted to the rank of major. During that same weekend I had a military attache visiting me, Colonel Bogdan Pilot, from the Polish embassy. He and his family spent a few days with me, and I was pleased that Colonel Pilot wanted to accompany me to the promotion ceremony where I functioned as chaplain.

As we approached the university, Colonel Bogdan asked me to stop so he could buy flowers for the new major's wife, and he bought a dozen beautiful red roses.

During the ceremony he offered them to the new major's wife, and the roses impressed the officers and the family of the promoted officer. They expressed their pleasure at this foreign custom.

Also during the ceremony, Colonel Robert Argonne welcomed the attache to the military science family of the university. In my remarks I made a connection between the Polish heroes who died for this country and those who served so well.

Following the ceremony, I spent the last day with my Polish friends in the Amish country. I needed a bigger car, as mine is very small. A friend, funeral director Terry O'Leary, allowed me to use his van. I was afraid because I had never driven a van before, but since the colonel was a pilot, I was happy to let him drive. Neither of us wanted to show that he was afraid to drive.

We enjoyed the Amish countryside, and when we returned, we had a big turkey dinner which we all enjoyed.

Unfortunately, shortly after my Polish friends left, I received some sad news. The first bishop to welcome me to Hopeland had died. I had a deep love and respect for him. His kindness and smiling face had reassured me that I would be fine and would be happy in Hopeland.

A year before, I had had breakfast with him and autographed one of my books for him. We discussed memories and enjoyed the humorous events of the past. When I said good-bye to my friend, I had a feeling that I would not see him again. He asked me to pray for him if he preceded me in going to Heaven.

I could not attend the funeral because it was too far away, but from where I am, I offered a special mass for my friend.

I am so sorry that another friend, Monsignor Edward Sweeney, also died. He had been twice offered a bishopric, which he turned down because he wanted to work at the parish level. He was chancellor for many years. Monsignor Edward Sweeney was one of the first priests to welcome me to this country. Neither could speak the other's language, though we used some Latin. After ten months and while visiting Hopeland, I felt that I should ask that the visit end and that I should be assigned to a parish.

Monsignor Edward asked me if I was being paid by my present pastor, and I told him that the pastor where I was staying wanted to keep me for three years without pay because he would not be getting another assigned assistant.

I told the monsignor that, of the five dollars a day I got in stipend, four were taken for room and board and one was for the organist, not to mention my private lessons in English. I was miserable.

The monsignor called Bishop John Feldman to ask for his help.

"Johnny," he said, "please help this Polish priest to become established." Fortunately, the bishop was able to help me to get an assignment, and now these two men who were so helpful to me have died and were buried the same week.

This caused me to think about the fleeting time and to remember how God is reflected in His people and His loving care and kindness.

In the late hours on the eve of Corpus Christi, I returned to Richton after visiting relatives. One of them, Amy, a parish bookkeeper, celebrated her 65th birthday. I was very tired and went to sit down on the bench under the gazebo in the garden. I contemplated at the shrines of the Virgin Mary and St. Jude and prayed for Amy. She is a kind-hearted person and is always trying to help people.

While I sat there thinking about the day, I heard a car pull into the drive. My friend, Richard Kamien, stopped to see me. He slammed his car door and shouted to me as he walked back.

"Michael, are you there?" he shouted.

I invited him into the yard and offered him something cold to drink. Richard had just returned from visiting his relative and stopped to talk.

"Richard," I said, "I'm really glad to see you today, the Feast of Corpus Christi. I encouraged people to come and tried my best to get them to come for the 10:00 A.M. mass and procession. I wanted them to celebrate one of the greatest feasts in our church. I announced the celebration at all masses and encouraged them to come. I also wanted them to participate by buying one flower, if they could afford it, to decorate the church.

"I don't like to talk about money in the church, but I feel that it is symbolic to offer flowers or candles for important occasions so that the altar looks nice. Most of the time the response is good, and this time it was also good.

"One widow brought flowers from her yard. She is an immigrant who came to the United States with her son and husband. She had been in a labor camp where she was forced to learn Russian, so I often speak Russian to her.

"The flowers she had brought to the church were so precious, though some were the wild kind. There were also roses given by a young mother, Theresa Abbey. I knew that this young mother had a very difficult life. After being separated from her husband, she had been reunited with him in Germany, and she thought that, by offering the flowers, it would help in her reunion. I thought that, if even only these wild flowers adorned the altars, Jesus would be pleased. But there were also flowers left over from a recent funeral. The altars were beautiful, with the incense and the older gentlemen serving as altar boys.

"One of the gentlemen carrying the cross during the procession was too attached to the cross. He stood with it throughout the entire service. The other stood ready to assist me as I incensed the altar. We didn't have at the time even *one* altar *boy* to help serve.

"I sometimes tell the parishioners that I am used to saying mass by myself, but at the same time, I can't collect money, say mass, and play the organ all at the same time. However, I could attach bells to my shoes and ring them."

I continued, "I have to laugh sometimes; otherwise, I will suffer more than I do! But in my experience as a priest and from my background at the seminary, I acknowledge the importance of a feast like Corpus Christi, the Holy Eucharist—that's the reason that we commit ourselves to the priesthood.

"Didn't Jesus say, 'Go into the city... and follow a man... and he will show you an upstairs room, spacious and furnished and all in order'?

"Richard," I continued, "there is a strong demand from our Lord that the places where we celebrate the Holy Eucharist should be special places. There are many churches where people care how they are kept. But, Richard, there was something that upset me about that celebration. I told you that I encouraged people to come. The weather was beautiful, but where was everyone?"

"Don't tell me that. We all experience a drop in participation. But you were there, and a few Polish-American immigrants were there to sing," Richard remarked.

"So, Richard, should I feel sad? Wasn't I sent here to bless this small group? But why, if we are committed to our church, do the people take it all for granted?" I asked.

Richard said, "In my church we have a heavy mass schedule; we don't celebrate as elegantly as in the ethnic parishes, but we have great love."

"I know," I said, "territorial parishes are different. I miss the time when I lived among the Irish people, trying to praise God and serve them.

"Before you go, there is something else I'd like to talk to you about. Lately, I see that parents do not strongly encourage their children to come to C.C.D. classes. After they are confirmed, the parents no longer encourage them to continue their education in Church doctrine. But you know, that is wrong. We are obligated as adults to be educated in our faith. We see something when people come to baptize a child or to get married or even for a funeral; they know nothing about the mass. Even the basics are forgotten. Yet, they call themselves Roman Catholics.

"I encourage the people to send their children, including high school students, to classes. I instruct the converts personally. It is different to have personal contact with a priest. I think teaching is our privilege. Jesus said, 'Go and teach all the nations everything I taught you.' I think that people are taking their priests and their faith for granted, but how can I yell at the faithful who are there? I just wish more of them would be concerned about our ministry."

"There is only one solution," said Richard. "Let's say a prayer for our ministry. If people would pray more, maybe there would be more concern and more priests. Maybe God is giving a message about whether or not people care about their churches and to give an example to their children."

Richard and I prayed together and promised to meet again soon and sit and talk underneath the gazebo behind St. Agatha's.

These reflections are based on some disappointments that sometimes happen in a small ethnic parish. I feel that they should not be ignored.

I do not believe that it is the clergy who neglect, but it is a lack of support that occurs.

Most of my ministry deals with our parish, but my outreach ministry from time to time includes the military service to the future lieutenants.

I was extremely happy when I received a combat uniform from the Military Science Department at the university. When I wore it, some of the young people at the meeting said that I looked like one of them. I took it as a compliment and responded, "That's what I like to look like."

Then I started to wonder if there would be any occasion to wear it. Shortly after this joyful moment, there was an announcement on the television that the United States, with full cooperation of the United Nations, would send about twenty-eight thousand troops— marines, navy and army—to Somalia in Africa, where people were starving and where local authorities could not protect the good people who tried to deliver food and medical aid. They could not reach many people because of guerrilla warfare. The food was stolen and kept, so it did not reach its destination; therefore, the hungry did not get fed.

If there is a Christian country with a Christian attitude to love thy neighbor and to protect him and to defend him, such as in the case of Somalia, the United States should be commended for it. We really did follow the advice of our Lord, which is to love neighbors, which also means to sacrifice for them.

I mentioned this in the sermons after the announcement came, that people should pray with me for the best young people, officers, generals, and even the president of the United States, who try to help to restore order in the region of Somalia and allow the people to live, to eat, and not to die.

"Isn't it enough that three hundred thousand people already died of starvation and hundreds of children are dying every day," I said. The people of St. Agatha's prayed loudly and begged our Lord for protection of the troops in Somalia.

It is difficult not to be involved. We are concerned with our neighborhoods, our city and, of course, where we work. I feel obliged to help when I teach at the university. I am careful, however, not to be a religious adviser on the university campus, but when the situation occurs and a student approaches me and wants to talk about his personal problems, I listen. I always, in a positive way, try to cheer up the young person, the future intelligentsia of the United States. So even though I do not advise a large group, I am happy to be their private adviser.

Alfredo Morelli, a student from one of my classes, came to me and asked for my help.

"Father Michael, I really need to talk with you. Do you have a little time for me? I have a class in ten minutes, but on the way we could talk. You know that no one else will listen to me," he said.

"Of course I will."

Alfredo then said, "Father Michael, please believe me, I don't know how you did it when you were young like me. I know that you wanted to be a priest, so perhaps you didn't have the complications in your life like loving someone the way I do. My girlfriend walked out of my life around Christmastime. Here it is March, and I see no reason for trying to work hard and to study as I am becoming more and more depressed. What would you do? Please tell me."

We continued to walk toward the building where I taught my next class. Then I said to Alfredo, "First of all, you are at the university to study and not to complicate your life. And this serious business with your girlfriend or girlfriends should not be your primary concern, but to study and, again I am telling you, to study. My gosh, Alfredo, you help your parents by working hard and helping to pay for your tuition. This distraction can be very harmful to you if you allow it to continue."

I told Alfredo that he was intelligent, healthy and young, with possibilities for a great future in his profession, and that there was plenty of time for a serious relationship later.

Alfredo asked me what he should do to stop his worries and feelings about Anita Portian whom he could not forget. My solution was discipline, organization with class assignments, research, term papers, oral reports, or anything to keep himself busy. These should be of more concern than Anita. I reminded him that his time at school is limited to a few years.

Alfredo then asked me how I made it when I was a student at the seminary, working on my master's and for my Ph.D. I told him that I had no parents and no support, only a strong will to study. I suggested to Alfredo that he go through the book he had for his political science class, underlining and outlining names, dates, statistics and definitions, and that he should also write it out, or even maybe put it on tape so that he could listen to it instead of rock music while he was cleaning floors or washing dishes. He could even put the professors' lectures on tape, which would better prepare him for quizzes and tests.

"I'll try," said Alfredo. "Take care, Father Michael."

"See you on Friday when we have a quiz; be prepared, and I hope you get a good grade," I replied.

When the conversation ended, I went to my other class of Russian studies in Russian Conversation for advanced students.

Then I went on my way to pastoral visits of the sick. I stopped to pick up the Blessed Sacrament, and on my way, I prayed that God would inspire young American students to do their best in their spiritual and intellectual lives.

Soon school was over, and we got a long relaxing summer vacation. I enjoyed that time to renew myself and to enjoy the beauty of the outdoors.

However, after a long summer vacation, the semester began again. This time I would teach the second year of Russian. The course is very intense and covers the completion of grammar, more conversation, and translations.

As each new class begins, the students smile a little, look at me, and wonder what the priest/professor is going to tell them and how he will handle the lessons and instructions. They find out quickly that they will have to study. My syllabus states my policy and shows also that I am very well organized. I will try to help them learn a subject that is very difficult. Can you imagine how an American-born student with an Anglo-Saxon background will try to speak a Slavic language? Most of them do very well since they are usually conscientious students and hard workers.

Soon, the semester began to pass quickly, and I was invited again to perform chaplain service at the Military Department on the occasion of welcoming new cadets, a new chairman of the department, and a new colonel commander of the Reserve Officers Training Corps in the State of Ohio. Also in attendance were officers and cadets, with their wives and children, and university officials. I, in my colonel's uniform, was happy to perform in this service, to give the invocation and benediction. I also made a few remarks.

I pointed out to this group how beautifully American military and families are unified when they celebrate such an occasion. They deserve high commendation for creating such an atmosphere, and I asked God's blessing for long, healthy and happy lives for new lieutenants.

After so many activities in the parish, at the university, and in the army, I appreciate some peaceful time.

God spoke to the prophets in silence, though He may have appeared with majesty and might and in wind and lightning. But the encounter with the supernatural gave the prophets a taste of the tranquility of Heaven.

I realize that I am not a saint, but I try to obey and observe the precepts of the Church so that I can fulfill my duties. However, sometimes when I grow weary and before I burn out, I like to be alone.

I pray before the Blessed Sacrament in the church, and I sit alone in silence. It is also possible to find a peaceful corner in the yard where I can relax. But more than anything else, like most people, I feel best when I am close to my Lord.

There is a closeness between the Almighty and the humble. I try to be a mediator between God and His people and must be close to my Master in moments of silence.

When I studied at the University of Ottawa, my friend, the pastor where I was in residence, sometimes disappeared. I often wondered where he went. One day Father George Gilbride returned, and I asked him where he went. Father George took me to his office and explained how important it is for a priest to get away from his duties.

He had been to Florida for a few days. He said that life is only given once from God and it is good to escape stress before he breaks down. He went to the ocean to rest and to be close to God and His creations.

Later Father George became one of the bishops of Ottawa, and he often visited me at St. Agatha's.

So in moments of silence, I remember my dear friend. A few years ago he died. I pray for him.

Of all the others from Ottawa that I miss, some stand out more than others. Bishop George is one of them. He was an excellent preacher and very pious when he said mass, but sometimes he smiled during confirmation ceremonies. His miter and staff gave him an authoritative and powerful appearance. But, in private life, he was just George—brotherly, friendly, and ready to help his priests when they needed it.

He had a wonderful sense of humor. I remember one time that he asked me to bring to his place on a motorcycle another friend's wife when I came to visit. I asked him if he meant for me to travel that far with a woman. He replied, "She's an angel," and I knew that he was kidding me.

More than anything else George was my spiritual adviser and friend. When he died, I knew that I had lost my buddy.

Rosemary was married to one of George's good friends who had been a priest for many years. Bob, George's friend, had asked the pope for dispensation from the priesthood to marry. Prior to it he was asked to become a missionary bishop for the Eskimos. I blessed their marriage in a Toronto church.

Bob is a very good, intelligent person, and I had the opportunity to study with him while I was in Canada. Not only is he a good person, but he is also talented and was able to build his parents a home in Prince George Province.

Would he make a good husband? Of course, but I am certain that his flock misses him. Both he and Rosemary are well organized. When I visited them in Toronto, she told me where I was to sit at the table. The worst part was that she had promised me Irish potatoes with onions and gravy, but because I was late, she got upset and ate my potatoes.

She has a pleasant face and blond hair and is very pretty. Her clothes, however, reflect her background as a nun. More importantly she seems not to want the two of us to be friends anymore. I do not understand why she feels threatened by me. Perhaps she feels that I would try to get her husband to return to the priesthood or that I didn't like nuns.

There is a Polish proverb which says, "Speech is silver; silence is golden. Gold attracts people more than silver; it is more precious."

So, even in a small parish like St. Agatha's, there are a few corners where I can find tranquility and silence. In the shade of the trees, I feel comfortable. I planted them myself when they were small and watered and nurtured them. They have grown so much that I even have to trim them now. In their shade my soul and body rest.

The shrubbery must be trimmed, too; it takes time and energy. What used to be empty space is now, in times of sadness and depression, a shelter for me.

I like to beautify the place for my friends and for the birds and rabbits that still come to visit me from time to time to retrieve my carrots and cabbage.

Sometimes, *little bandits* intrude in *Father's* yard. Little kids jump over the fence. The security light scares them away, and barking dogs let me know that there is an intruder in my garden.

Many other incidents seem to occur in the everyday life of a priest. One beautiful June morning, even before I went to the church, I got a call from the deputy mayor. He wanted to know if I had seen the sign that had been installed in front of the church marking a pedestrian crossing. It had been restored after some teenagers ruined it with graffiti.

I had asked for the signs, and in two days they were installed. When Deputy Mayor Stazio called, he apologized for not returning my call asking for the signs.

"*I'm* really sorry for not calling *you* to thank you, but like most people, I take some things for granted," I said.

"That's okay. You know that I always try to help you and your parishioners," said Deputy Mayor Stazio.

"I will write a letter to you and your traffic officer. Your kindness will not be forgotten," I responded.

The people feel safer now coming to church. The curbs and sidewalks were also fixed by the city, and the street is paved. The city authorities also recognized the parish on the 75th anniversary of St. Agatha's. We should never take their care for granted, but it should be appreciated.

On many occasions the local bishop has come to my parish to celebrate, and this included the time when I celebrated my 25th anniversary in the priesthood. Often, he is also present for friendly lunches with people from the university, the city, or representatives from the Polish consul or visitors from Canada.

I appreciate Bishop Edward Sheridan's assistance for St. Agatha's and know that he also helps the other parishes. Since the bishop is in the same city, it is a good feeling to have someone like him nearby. I feel that is how it should be between bishops and priests, which is completely different in this country than it is in Poland.

There, bishops were known for their powers and splendor. I hope that they have changed their policy so they can approach their brother priests with love and support.

I often wonder how it is possible for a person to be lonely. I know that I cannot be lonely when so many people help me. There is more to be appreciated and not taken for granted. The university is related to the parish through my teaching there for the past seventeen years. I never expected to be close to its president and the other professors in the way that I am.

They come to visit and give me advice. The participate in Slavic evenings organized in the parish building because I am faculty adviser for the Slavic Society.

There is a mixture of friendships—the simplicity of Polish immigrants and their morals and my other friends who are students and professors. It is a good place for me to be.

I want to share my heritage with my parishioners. They are generous with donations and kindness, even with advice, and sometimes they even help with the upkeep of the church property.

Often there are funny incidents in the life of a parish priest, even though they do not start out that way. One morning when I went to church, I noticed that there was a fountain of water in front of the church where there hadn't been one before. I certainly didn't remember any project that would cause all this mud and water. It looked as if a water pipe had burst. So, I thought it would be easy to get it fixed; all I had to do was to call the city water department. I did, but no answer. I then tried to call the deputy mayor's office, but no answer there either. I even tried to call the deputy mayor at his home, but still no one answered. Where could everyone be? I knew that it wasn't a holiday, so where was everyone? Then, I decided to try to find someone to rescue me from this dilemma, and I got into my car, put on my emergency lights, and drove as fast as I could downtown to City Hall. I even hoped that a policeman would stop me so I could have him get me there faster. I finally reached the city building and parked in a reserved space. I figured that, if I had to pay for a ticket for illegal parking, they would excuse it because it was an emergency.

It was ten o'clock in the morning when I arrived, but every door of the building was closed and locked! Maybe someone would come soon and open up the building. Soon, people started to arrive and stand in line, also hoping to get into the building.

One gentleman standing in line asked me to give a sermon, so I entertained people as we waited. Finally, a policeman came by, and we learned that it was the day of the city picnic. Everyone, including the service personnel, was at the picnic.

One person asked if I was going to take up a collection after the sermon, but I said that I only wanted to learn how to swear. Then I asked if someone would teach me, as I was thinking about the water problem we had at the church.

Soon the people who had gathered started to recite religious slogans, such as *Alleluia, praise be to God*.

About that time another policeman stopped. He recognized me and asked what was the matter. I told him about the serious water problem, how there was no one in the city building to help and now the people were asking me to preach.

One of the gentlemen asked me why I didn't know how to swear, and then he said, "I want to join your temple; I like the way you talk."

I explained to the man that I was assigned to a church and that I was a priest, but that he was welcome to come worship with my congregation anytime he wanted.

Finally, the officer told me that there should be someone at the water department, which was located elsewhere, but when I got there, only a person talking on the telephone was there. I waited while he talked, and talked, and talked. After about a half an hour, I knocked on the window and shouted, "It's an emergency! My church will be flooded!"

At last someone promised to send someone to help, so I returned to St. Agatha's.

Finally, someone came to disconnect the water. St. Agatha's was built in 1925, and the place where the water meter is located was full of mud and stones. We tried to clean out the mud and take it to the dumpster, but it was hot and humid and the mud was very difficult to carry.

The next day the men from the water department tried to remove the old pipes, and there was still water and mud. One of my friends arranged a meeting with someone from the water department, and they donated a new water meter and advised me as to what I should do. I also found out that, since the water had not gone through the meter, the church would not be billed for the lost water.

The water meter was located beneath the sidewalk, so Anthony Rialto, a friend and supervisor in the water department, had to come up for air once in a while. He was also working on Sunday because this was an emergency. People coming to church were shocked when they saw a head pop out of the sidewalk. They looked at what was going on, and when they saw what was being done, they sympathized with Anthony as it was a very hot day. When the meter was finally installed, I was so relieved. But, something good happened. Good people helped me. I really did not realize when I was in the seminary that I would have to deal with all of these odd things. I soon learned what it means to be an administrator of a parish.

When it was all over, with dirty hands, filthy shirt, and my priestly collar that I retrieved from the mud, I entered the church and thanked God for relieving my stress because of this dangerous situation.

In the meantime, I received a letter from the bishop congratulating me on the publication of my new book. In my books, *A Touch of Divinity* and *Beauty of Creation*, I try to show an appreciation for the beauty of nature and the support of my friends and superiors. I was very happy that the bishop was pleased that I use my time creatively. I had notified the bishop when my book was published because I felt that I should. I remember when nothing could be published without the approval of church authorities.

Sometimes, our days are not what we would like them to be. Once, when I needed to go to the bank, I went to the garage to get the car, but I couldn't get the door open because of the thunderstorm that had occurred during the night. There had been weeks when there was no rain, but now this storm caused some damage in the city. It happened about one o'clock in the morning and woke me up. This storm reminded me of one I went through while I lived in Poland. Entire villages were destroyed. I remember how the lightning lit up the sky and the frightened animals ran to the barn for shelter. It was so bad that the local priests and nuns lit pastoral candles and asked God to stop the terrible disaster in the villages.

Even when the children went to the orphanage for school the next day, they could smell the burning the lightning had done the night before.

Recalling this, I prayed, "May God have mercy on His creation and not punish us."

So, on this night when the lightning was stronger than it had been before, I knew that something had been hit. I prepared for the antenna which was located on the roof to be hit, but I didn't know that a remote control door opener could be affected. I had to have the destroyed part replaced and installed.

Also, because of the storm, I was going to be late going to the bank on parish business. Many of the roads were closed due to the storm, but I was able to make my way toward my destination. As I approached one corner, a young woman stopped me and asked me if I could take her to the hospital because her baby was due any minute. I wasn't sure if I should help because I remembered a time when I went to the aid of someone near the church and I almost got killed.

It happened one night that a couple had stopped near the church, and I thought that perhaps the woman might be sick and need help. As I approached the fence surrounding the parking lot, I called out and asked them if they needed help. The man, who had gotten out of the car, jumped over the fence and ran toward me with a hunting knife. I grabbed the man's hand and averted being hit in the face, but was wounded on my arm. The man robbed me of my salary and threw my wallet to the ground. Then he ran to the car, and they drove away, leaving me bleeding in the parking lot. I couldn't even see because my glasses had been knocked off and were broken.

So, now I am careful about helping people, but I felt terrible about not helping a pregnant woman because it goes against my nature.

When I finally got to the bank, some men stopped me and said that there had been a robbery. Because the president of the parish council worked there, they let me pass.

I went upstairs and told her that the bank had been robbed. Then I realized that, if I had been on time, she would probably have been downstairs and would have been a witness or, even worse, a hostage.

Much later I went to lunch with a friend, Gregory North, who has been a pastor for twenty-five years at a church which is close to the downtown area. We met at a restaurant near Chippewa Lake, a beautiful location, but it looks like the boondocks.

While driving to the Oaktree Restaurant, I kept laughing to myself because there were no signs or directions to help me find my way in this wilderness.

The restaurant was in a very old building made of wood and in dire need of some repair work to the windows and doors. However, the main door was made of steel, which indicated that even in the wilderness there are bandits.

Because of the heavy traffic on the road, I was late for the meeting with my friend and the others who were in attendance.

Upon my arrival, I was cordially welcomed, and my friend treated me to a Black Russian and we toasted the big boss.

Sitting at the table next to Father Gregory North, we both evaluated the situation of the Church today. It seems that we were both skeptical of the recent approval by the Vatican to have girls serve at the altar.

"See, Michael, there were suspicions and troubles when there were boys serving. What about the girls?" he asked.

I responded, "It doesn't matter to me. So much has happened since Vatican II, so what's new?"

I then told Father Gregory that I don't have to start something in the parish that I know will not work and that my quiet sensible parish will not accept altar girls.

We continued our discussion about how children today are not as willing as they used to be to prepare themselves for First Communion, when they will receive Jesus into their hearts and minds for the first time, and how from time to time some of them find excuses not to attend instructions because they have to distribute newspapers or practice for some sport or dance classes. They even talk so emphatically about it like it was the end of the world.

"Oh, yes, Father Gregory, it is true that they act like pagans and not Christians who were baptized."

We both agreed that not only priests and teachers, but parents, too, are responsible for the religious education of children.

The little, husky and strong-looking Father Gregory looked out toward the lake and said, "God have mercy on us and save us from going back to paganism."

After the dinner was over, I had to return home. I had enjoyed the meal and the conversation, but as I drove back, I wondered about what we had discussed. Somehow I felt a little better that I was not the only one who sees these situations not changing for the better, but for the worse. However, there is still hope because the Holy Spirit oversees the Church and many devoted people.

5

Prayers and Retreats Help to Overcome Extreme Difficulties

———◦◦◦———

We do not have too much choice when we get an assignment, nor do we get a choice of neighbors. We have to experience unusual situations when we live in a high crime area. Part of the neighborhood of St. Agatha's is no exception, but due to a strong faith, through prayer, through renewal, and through retreats, it is easier to overcome difficulties in our lives.

Not far from Richton, the Jesuit fathers have a retreat house. Loyola of the Lakes is situated south of the city, and the chapel is situated in such a way that people can go there by themselves for spiritual directions or for retreats under the direction of Jesuits in that area.

I wanted to take a few days for a retreat before the Fourth of July. I knew at this time that there was almost no one there at the nearby retreat house because so many rooms were empty and the corridors were deserted. I realized that the quiet nights would afford me the opportunity for prayer, reflection, and meditation, as well as for the rest that I needed. The roads were lined with pine and maple trees and gave people a shady place to walk after meditations and meals. The Stations of the Cross are beautifully situated among the bushes. They remind us of the Lord's passion and suffering. After this reflection, we can ask ourselves, "How can we complain, after our Archpriest, Jesus, was rejected and suffered as He did?"

The chapel is located on a hill and at the bottom of that hill are beautiful statues of our Lady of Fatima and the children to whom she appeared.

Before the sun began to set, I liked to sit down on a bench in front of the statues to finish my evening prayer. For a moment, I noticed two rabbits who seemed to be kneeling in front of the statues. Their large ears moved when I sneezed. They approached very close to me, which suggested that the people at the retreat house are gentle with the animals there. At that moment, I didn't feel lonely in this open space, and I was glad that I was not alone praying, but had the company of the sweet little rabbits.

Another time, while I was walking the stations and praying, a big black dog ran toward me. I wasn't sure if I should pet him, but when he drew near, I spoke to him. "Be good. I love you, but don't bite me because I don't taste good." The dog turned around several times and left. I later found out that the dog belonged to the Jesuit fathers. I thought that this is why the dog doesn't hurt people attending the retreats because the fathers have trained it well.

The evenings at the retreat house are especially quiet for guests. There were two fathers who ate supper and shared the conversation with me. I told them that I liked the privacy at the house and the people who work there. I saw that their commitment was genuine, and I appreciated being there and away from the everyday duties.

The three days and two nights passed quickly in these beautiful surroundings, and when it was time to leave, I stopped at the chapel and asked God for guidance with my pastoral ministry. I left the place feeling stronger, healthier, and eager to continue my commitment to do my best, counting on God and my friends to help me in this ministry.

After my retreat, I remembered that God, my friends, and I are all important, but to appreciate the generosity and kindness of our friends, we must examine our neighborhoods. The truth is that they are not clean or safe. For instance, one evening after mass, I rested a moment. Just as dinner was about ready, the phone rang; it was an elderly parishioner, crying and very excited.

"Father," she cried, "there is no one here to listen to my problems."

I asked her to please continue, even though dinner was ready and would no doubt get cold before the woman finished her conversation. I asked her what was wrong.

"Father, I used to go shopping with my husband, but since he died, I go by myself. Tonight as I was coming back to the car after wandering around the shopping mall after I had finished shopping, there stood a young man by my car. He pushed me into the car when I opened the door and punched me in the face. I tried to defend myself, but he grabbed my purse and ran away. Father, I am sad, as this has never happened to me before and I am afraid. Please pray for me," Helen said.

I promised to pray for her, and I also tried to cheer her up, encouraging her to count the many good things that have happened to her in her life.

Though time passed I could not forget the elderly lady's ordeal. I sat down; dinner was cold by now. I remembered more abuses that I had seen in the past twenty years in this neighborhood. I remembered the professor from Richton University who visited me when I first arrived at St. Agatha's. That visit almost cost the professor his life.

In the middle of the street directly in front of the church, he was stopped by a young person who pointed a gun at his window and asked him to get out and give him the car. The professor turned into the parking lot and ran to the rectory. He called the police and gave them a description of the assailant, but after the police came, they were not ever able to find the man. The feeling of powerlessness and neglect remained with the professor. I really felt sorry for him.

I also remember another time when two girls were stopped in front of the church by others of a gang. They were beat up, and the other girls tried to pull out their hair. Neighbors across the street were sitting on their porch, but they did not want to get involved so no one called the police; therefore, incidents such as these are never resolved.

Another time I recall that two elderly sisters living on the next street over were attacked and raped by a young man. One was killed and the other taken to the emergency room. Why would anyone want to hurt an eighty year old woman who lived peacefully in the neighborhood?

Fortunately, witnesses of this incident took the criminal's license number, and he was arrested, convicted, and sentenced to eight to fifteen years in jail.

One pious Italian lady who used to come to St. Agatha's was stopped in front of the statue of our Lady by a pimp who was driving his big Cadillac. He jumped out, threw her to the ground, grabbed her purse, and beat her with a pistol. The people who were waiting outside for mass were scared because they thought that he would use the pistol on them. Again, the police were unable to do anything.

Whenever one of these incidents occurred, I went to my room and prayed. I often become so sad about these occurrences that I looked at my Winchester rifle and asked myself how I could protect myself and my parishioners with this lethal weapon. Psychologically, the presence of this weapon helped me to feel at home. On my knees, I prayed to God that my parishioners would be protected against the young healthy criminals who sometimes commit such terrible crimes in their neighborhood. I was sure that my prayers would be answered.

Through the years I observed that many good things happen—blessings from God and the administration of Sacraments for the people. Now I am not so sure.

The pockets of my pants and jackets used to be empty, but now they are more and more full of many different kinds of keys—keys to the church, keys to the rectory, to the other parish buildings, and also to the garages. What is this multitude of keys telling us? You don't trust people as much as you used to when, as clergy, we have to lock the buildings and gates to protect everything. We always have to check to see if everything is locked up safe because of the terrible evil in the world. People today do not even have sacred places like churches and synagogues. That worries me. Why must I lock it, unlock it, turn the alarm system on, and also have lights that illuminate the church property?

I see from time to time that there is no light in the hearts and minds of thieves, bad teenagers, and other bad elements in many countries and also in this beautiful land—that light which enlightens our minds and hearts to work hard and to study and not to steal, but to respect not only sacred places, but also our neighbors.

I thought that it would at least be safe outside and inside the church, especially in the sanctuary near the Tabernaculum. But it wasn't so. Three times, young teenagers tried to open the most holy place, the Tabernaculum. Evidence was found all over the church, vestments on the floor and the Tabernaculum scratched. Even the most holy place was abused because of a lack of respect. The teenagers appear from outside the neighborhood, and police cannot seem to help. It was suspected that they were under the age of eighteen, but no one knows for sure.

But ethnic groups can also cause problems. There are small groups or cliques in the neighborhood, and if something doesn't work for them or they just don't like something, they can harm others, including the pastor of the church. They should show respect for others and approach strangers more gently. God forbid if an incoming pastor eliminated services in the language of the parish, even if there is only a small group who use it. They deserve to be given service in their own language. They like to sing, listen to the sermon and pray together in the language of their child-hood. It reminds them of their homeland.

I received a phone call from my friends who are now living in Delaware; they said they were happy because they could attend a church with the same name as the one they left here in Richton, St. Agatha. However, a new pastor, an American-born priest, announced shortly after his arrival that he was going to cancel the Polish masses because there was more money donated at the English masses.

I was very sad. Even though it was quite a distance away, I told my friends that it was terrible that money was the determining fac-tor in a church where it had been the Polish people who had built and supported the church for so long. As long as the founders are living, the clergy owes them a lot, and the least that can be done for them is to say masses and give sermons in their native language.

We should reflect on the terrible businesslike situation which is becoming more and more common in the life of the Christian churches. Isn't the spirit more important than the flesh? Most importantly, we know that we were not ordained to be businessmen, but to proclaim the Good News from Heaven, one of love and sal-vation for all mankind. That is the most important issue in our lives. We also believe that God will not abandon the priest, will not let him go hungry, homeless or poor. He abundantly grants daily bread and the material needs of the priest and of his parish. It has been true for two thousand years, that the Church is proclaiming the Good News/Gospel today, as Christ proclaimed it yesterday, that the Church will survive and God's people will be cared for.

But sometimes even a priest gets tired. I often think to myself, "I am tired; I am just a human being." But it was a joy to see people in the church for the seventeen masses that I said for the weekends of the Christmas and New Year's season. It helped me when I real-ized that the people need me.

At the same time, I wonder how the future will be if the younger generation doesn't bother to learn the simple prayers and to respect religious people and the elderly around them.

I recall one evening visiting some friends. I had blessed their children in the hospital after complicated births. I had not seen them for a while, but when I saw their smiling faces, I kissed and hugged them. Today, *Fluffy*, and the oldest, *Pinky*, are healthy, beautiful, and intelligent, and I hope they will always be religious. During the visit, I learned that the oldest was going to receive First Communion, and as a priest, I was very happy because I know that Jesus will be in her heart, her mind, and her life.

Fluffy is a little troublemaker. She likes to fight, but from time to time when she looks at me with those dark eyes, I realize that God has created a beautiful creature.

Parents should be blessed abundantly for their total devotion to these lovely creatures. They were not sure that the children would be healthy, but they are. I consider this a miracle. I often think about them and keep them in my heart with a priestly love for them. When I am asked to visit them, I gladly go.

I wish that all families would take care of their children like the parents of Fluffy and Pinky do. They are obedient and accept their parents' advice quietly and seriously. That particular evening was important to me as much so as the day of the Nativity of our Lord.

Jesus especially loved children. He told the apostles, "If you want to enter the kingdom of heaven, then you shall become like little children."

Christmas passed and New Year's came and went, and I was grateful to God for all my caring friends, even though I still remember the rejection I felt when I first arrived. However, I feel that the people and I are successfully praising God and keeping up a nice place to worship. Still, I wonder why we must be afraid and if fear is justified.

Sometimes I have unusual visitors. This time it was Maria and Thaddeus Morski. They came because of a previous meeting.

Maria seemed interested in my background and, after listening to my stories, asked for copies of my two books. But then she disappeared, and I didn't see her for a while. I called her and told her that her autographed books were waiting for her. Finally, Maria and Thaddeus, who are Polish, arrived. I thought this would be a short conversation, but they talked about their Polish-American background for hours. I soon began to realize that they wanted to be friends. Maria is also a candidate for confirmation and will soon be confirmed with a small group of young people at St. Agatha's.

When my new friends left, I finished my evening prayers and went to sleep. I don't believe in dreams, but this evening, my dream was terrifying. I was at the home of my distant uncle in Hopeland, and as the door was opening, I saw a group of unusual people. Their faces were unfriendly, and they held tools like weapons and handguns. They didn't look like they wanted to talk to me. I was afraid that something tragic would happen to my relatives and to their property. These people were dressed in very colorful clothing and had punk haircuts. In the dream they ran across the street, broke a big window, jumped inside and began to destroy the furniture. The flames from the fire they started came through the roof, and they sneered at me as they looked at me. I asked them not to destroy anything, but they ignored me.

I woke up to what I thought was the phone, but I couldn't reach it in my dream. It was not the alarm clock, but it was the high school students who were walking past the house, screaming and yelling. I was afraid they were going to damage the church property as they had done before. I heard their vulgar language, and it was language I had not heard even from the Communists or men in the army.

I sat and wondered at the coincidence between my dream and reality. But reality is not a dream, and a dream only happens off and on. In reality, these children behave like this every day.

In the church I thanked God that the dream was not reality. I walked around the church and talked with a woman who was walking her dog. As I locked the doors, I told her that I wished that I could leave the building unlocked, but I knew that the children who walk by every day respect nothing, and that they would do some damage to the church if it was left unlocked.

I began to talk with Irena Komus, the woman who was walking with me. "You look a little scared; I know you are vulnerable," I said.

"I think that, at the same time the president goes to foreign countries surrounded by secret service men, there is fear in this country. Something should be done so people can live without fear. Those who are on welfare and not working do not help the problem. Not to mention, the United States spends millions to help countries when something should be done here. For example, billions of dollars go to other countries, but only one million would help our neighborhood. Cultural centers could be built. I was even advised not to go to some of the parks without an armed guard. If there was special education for parents on how to raise babies, maybe there would not be such problems with young, healthy men and women who do not want to work or who cannot read and write. You even see them downtown. It is a terrible waste of talent.

"I am not prejudiced; I am part of a minority group myself. I don't remember poor people coming from Eastern Europe being supported by welfare and receiving food stamps. One of the conditions for coming to this country is that we not apply for welfare or food stamps. I have worked mentally and physically, not only for the spiritual needs of my people, but for the upkeep of the property."

Irena responded, "You probably don't remember, but President Johnson, despite his politics, had good intentions. But, somehow society ignores this condition, where there is child abuse, rape, murder and conditions below the poverty level."

I had to agree.

As we walked and talked, another friend came up to us and asked what we were discussing.

"I think I will run for mayor," I said.

"Will you create a safe city for us?" she asked. "God forbid I will meet some young man on the street with unpleasant ideas in his head, but I must walk to visit an old friend and help to take care of her."

Finally, the three of us finished our discussion. We agreed we should keep our faith and survive our fears. But I said that faith without action is dead. We agreed to get together again and that people should be educated, and hoped that there would be a president who would encourage the young people not to waste their talents. The same people who can sing and dance beautifully can also learn to read, write, and work hard at a job. We also decided that some of the foreign aid sent out of this country could help to improve things here.

124

Often, the everyday reality in the pastoral ministry and the administration of the parish indicates that there are many details not only to remember, but many things to carry out.

When the pastor reflects on spiritual needs, he needs to remember his parishioners and the doctrines and sacraments that are important to them. I enjoy officiating at these services and celebrations, such as Baptisms, First Communions, Confirmations, and Marriages. There is always the preparation of those who participate that brings them closer to God and the Church. Sometimes the one who is involved does not take the sacraments seriously; therefore, what is considered a lifelong commitment becomes only a short participation.

Some of the Church's policies have changed. For example, the Church has taken a more liberal view of marriage annulments that has resulted in a stronger family life and love for the marriage partners.

When I was a little boy in the orphanage, I heard terrible stories from other children about how the parents fought with each other and sometimes even abused the children. I feel that children, in a very honest and simple way, related their frightening experiences where there was a lack of love. These children talked, and the others of us listened. I learned so much from these orphans. Even though these stories were of tragedy, sometimes they were of forgiveness and peacefulness, too.

Through all the ceremonies, people give of themselves to the parish. In the harmony of the liturgy, there is singing and organ music and there is praise for God, fulfillment of obligations and receiving new Sacraments.

Without faithful participation, the Church would be dead. The Tabernaculum, where Jesus is locked, requires special attention and honor. It is an honor to be able to care for the church and participate in the many Sacraments.

Going back to the spiritual leadership, I realize that a person's spiritual life starts in baptism and continues throughout childhood and old age, when the comfort of the Church is given as we approach death.

For the most part people care about the priests who are in charge of the churches they support. Clergy also need the advice of their peers. Encouraged by the local ordinary bishop and parish council, a priest is an important asset.

These people are my right hand. Throughout the past years, the meetings have been pleasant. They openly discuss matters concerning the spiritual and material welfare of St. Agatha's.

Some parishioners' experiences in some organizations are good. Their ideas and advice are very helpful, and I take their knowledge into account and try to cooperate with the parish council. I anxiously await the monthly meetings. All the meetings start and end with prayer and with the best intentions to do the best for God's glory and for the parishioners.

I do not like to hear people talk about parishes as small businesses. Perhaps seminarians do not realize what reality involves. I know how things are run and what the parish is really like. Life makes demands that are often beyond our ability to do well, and one must be prudent.

I realize that even the offices of the Church are bureaucratic, and directors and chairmen have ideas with which they annoy the poor, small parish priest. There are many retreats, activities, meetings and social gatherings. I question even the local bishop about what has happened with the Roman Catholic Church.

The answer is simple. "This is the new way of doing things. This is the situation that we have to work with," one of the bishops responded.

Sometimes I wonder, "How can I be at a retreat and, at the same time, take care of sick people? How can I attend a meeting when the garbage must be picked up and leaves piled around the buildings? How can I attend activities of the neighboring churches when I must be in my own church to hear confessions and say mass?"

As I wonder about the business of the Church, I also think of how different everything is from when I first became a priest in Poland. There, having a car, for example, seemed almost a luxury; here it is a necessity. Driving a car in the United States is a very crucial matter.

I remember that I then drove a small Polish two-cylinder; it was a good car and served me well because I lived fourteen kilometers from the grocery store and had to travel to eight elementary schools where I taught religion to the parish children.

Not all the driving experiences have been exciting for me. For instance, I went to visit my friend and newly appointed pastor at Our Lady of Good Counsel in Hopeland during the preparation for the Christmas holidays. As I drove, I kept thinking about the terrible driving conditions in Ohio.

Finally, after thinking of all the accidents that occur during the winter, I could see the church ahead. Unfortunately, as I arrived, there was a funeral procession in the parking lot. The entrance to the front of the church was blocked, so I had to back my car up. It just so happened that through my meditations I saw in the rearview mirror a horrible looking driver with sunglasses and a long beard bump into the rear of my car. I was not backing up too fast, so there was no damage done, only a scratch. The driver apologized and asked me not to call the police, and then he disappeared quickly.

This incident motivated me to drive even more carefully. I want to let everyone know that we should all drive with more caution, and in case of an accident, do not let the other driver leave without calling the police. There could be repercussions.

As I drove back to my home, I prayed to God and St. Christopher to help keep safety on the streets. I would remind my congregation about the trials of driving in America.

Sometimes I think that I worry too much, not just about the other drivers, but also about how poorly the teenagers treat the older people in the community. Even if I mention this in one of my sermons, I feel guilty that I have said something bad about the young people. But what happened one night on television really shook me up and surprised me, too. It was on a TV program that they recounted the experiences from fifty schools from around the country regarding the problems teachers face in the classroom. The program showed children carrying guns and knives to school. It also drew attention to the fact that children were fighting in and out of the classroom. One youngster was sentenced to two hundred years in prison for killing a substitute teacher and shooting the principal of the school. Of course, at the time he was sentenced, he said that he felt sorry and told the other children not to do what he had done, but it was too late. He said that he had always felt like killing someone, and now he doesn't know why he did it.

It was sad to watch this review of the behavior of the children in school. All of this was recorded on hidden cameras. All of the teachers were powerless while the children danced, jumped up and down, bothered others, made faces and did everything except listen and pay attention to the teacher.

One principal of one of the schools who was on the program even said that she is not only afraid as a principal, but also as a private person. She became very emotional, started to cry, and asked that the interview be stopped for a moment. What a sad commentary!

After seeing this program, I became very angry and wanted to scream, asking God to have mercy on us. In this country that we love so much, why can a youngster in the sixth grade buy a gun and a child of six bring a pistol to school to protect himself from others?

I felt after watching this that I needed to remind the parishioners of the obligation we all have to be good parents and to pray to the King of the Universe for the children and that parents will pay more attention to their children, love them, and take care of them, also that they should teach their young people to respect life and not to kill.

The following Monday evening, I said mass for the children of C.C.D. classes as I do from time to time. After confessions and when mass started, I felt great watching the children with their teachers, parents, grandparents, and I started to breathe easier and think better about the children.

Not long after this I met Father Richard Longstone, an old friend, whom I had not seen for some time, and he asked me how I was doing with my pastoral ministry. Father Richard is a successful pastor in a large city parish; he has two assistants, a parish school and, of course, a wealthy neighborhood surrounding it. From time to time he likes to visit some of his friends, and so he decided to visit me this time. I was happy to see him and he certainly came at a good time to ask me how I was doing.

First of all, I told him that, every day for about three years when I said mass, I had some people attending for whose intention the mass was being said, and they were kind and good. I don't have an organist play every day. I also keep the windows open so the people could hear the birds singing in the spring or fall. One would expect that the church would be quiet and peaceful during mass, but there is always some disturbance made by the little children. I try to be compassionate and I realize that I should not mind these little annoying noises, but they do bother me.

"Father Richard," I said, "I am telling you, it is difficult to understand why God allows some disruptive situations to occur in the church."

Father Richard listened patiently while I continued.

I said, "Father Richard, believe me, I have missed the peace and silence for these past few years.

"Certainly the world is different. When I was a student in high school, I wondered if intelligence is achieved due to education or experience. At the seminary, Professor Marian Moony said it was also an adjustment to society and to culture and that this adjustment was very important. Education helps to develop intelligence, and the success or failure of using one's intelligence also figures in.

"I see how much the world has changed. I remember when people, even when they suffered, complained less. Families and nations used to be more united. In a way, they were happier and more satisfied. Once there was a time when most people did not accept liberal ideas about politics, religion, and education, but maybe the turmoil they went through during World War II caused psychological pain and problems. Maybe this is one of the reasons that people ran away from God at the time when so many suffered and were persecuted, executed, and burned in concentration camps. Even though faith became weak for many, both Christian and Jew, some maintained their strong faith in God and did not blame the heavens for earth's misery.

"In reality, there is a tremendous cultural change on all continents. Today, for someone like me, the adjustment to liberal ways of thinking in religion and politics is difficult. But the positive side to the painful experiences of war is always there. Good people search for ideas and want to discover the supernatural; perhaps some are sick and tired of the liberal views. Many want to go back to God and to interpret His kindness and compassion in more positive ways to the masses of people.

"The positive view is that, now, people are better off than they have ever been, at least in many countries. In many Western countries people have democracy and equal opportunities.

"These changes in the past years have also touched millions of Eastern European countries. When I was a young soldier in Russia, the churches were museums; people did not worship God during Stalin's time. Now, their democracy has given independence to many, though they are united in a commonwealth.

"It is very significant that a great number of people are still under Communist rule today, but the collapse of some Communist states indicates that the denial of God creates a revolution against the terror that reigned for seventy years.

"How will the Church adjust to today's situation? There is good news from Poland. I learned that the Catholic Church in that country has committed $700,000 for the victims of the Chernobyl disaster. This was an act of charity to the previous enemies of the Polish state. I was also heartened to learn that Polish priests are encouraged by their bishops to learn the Russian language in order to act as missionaries to Russia to instruct and to bring the Sacraments to the Russian people. They will also be able to help the Orthodox Church.

"I also observed that there are priests in the Russian parliament and that maybe their advice will help build a better future for their country. I thought that, if I were younger, I would be encouraged to go there and teach literature and language.

"In reality, now that I am here in the United States and my roots are very deeply implanted here, I see no reason to go to Eastern Europe. I also feel that I am needed here and want to continue in the pastoral ministry, teaching, writing, and serving in the U.S. Army.

"I know that there are many positive examples in my life and of many people throughout the world. I strongly believe that we will never stop searching for friendship and unity among all people.

"I realize that, even when there are good things going on in our lives, we still get hurt, though it may be unintentional.

My brother priest, friend, and spiritual director, whose advice was simple—*Take it easy, as we say in English*—helped me most by simply listening and giving good advice.

On a beautiful spring day I looked around while traveling from place to place on my visitations and saw the unusually colorful flowers and the sun shining after the previous day's rain. Around my neck, near my heart, I carry the Holy Communion for the people who are waiting for this service. As much as I watch the road, my mind works to acknowledge the great privilege to be a servant for God and to save the people whom God created.

But as always, reality prevails. I was very happy and thankful to God as I prayed, "Eternal Father, I know you love us. I am one of your creatures; I belong to you. You chose me to be your apostle, to proclaim your Gospel. Please help me to do the best in my ministry.

"I realize the importance of my legacy as a priest and a teacher, but above all, I consider myself a simple parish priest and human being. So, help me, God, to count the graces and blessings that you have granted me these many years as a priest."

One of the most important of these is that for the past twenty years I realized how much I could share with my fellow American brothers and sisters, to tell them how great it is to be free, not to be followed by the police, not to be suspected of political opposition, not to have to carry a passport, and to have equal privileges and opportunities. I tell them that life is good in America; all those facilities, such as hot water and electricity and even a car, are things that others in the world do not have, and we take them for granted. While meditating I thank Heaven that I am able to contact Jesus and carry His message to the people for whom I was ordained.

One of the first stops was to visit, in a gentle way, a tough parishioner, Mary Baker, who is almost one hundred years old. She always tries to do something to promote the culture of her fatherland. And that day she mentioned, "I still want to see children in the parish sing Polish songs and to learn Polish language and dances."

I understood how she felt, but I replied, "Mary, it is nobody's fault that ethnic parishes are becoming Americanized and changing their character. Really, there is not a lot of need for kids to continue to learn the language of their grandparents. I wonder if they could have the time to study something extra."

Of course, I am very concerned about Mary Baker's background and my own, too, but I am intelligent enough to realize that adjustments to America are a prime obligation and condition which was given to me by the diocesan authorities.

While continuing my journey with Jesus from place to place, I stopped at a very well-known parishioner's house, one that I have visited for many years. Some poor parishioners are paralyzed and unable to get out of their beds. As I distribute Communion, I see the loving care of a spouse, parent, or child. I express my sympathy each time I visit, but there is nothing else I can do except offer my prayers. What amazes me is that neither the patient nor the caregiver complains. The worst is when the patient says that he wants to die. This is so sad.

When they say that they want to die, I try to console them and say, "Life is a treasure given to us by God, and He must have a place for us in His Divine Providence. Perhaps He has plans that we do not even know about."

I remember very well, when I was twenty-one years old and collapsed from weakness caused by exhaustion, I found myself in the hospital, and as I lay in bed, I heard the doctors talking. This was the first sign in my life that I may not even survive one year, let alone ten years. I, too, felt very depressed, so I can understand how these old and bedridden people feel.

From time to time when I am lonely, I look at the books and remember my subject and that I studied the great knowledge of the Slavic nations.

The human mind is capable of memorizing, composing and writing poems, stories, and histories, as well as novels. These are human activities. It can be done if there is determination to do something else than just complain about the pain, sorrow, and daily suffering we encounter in our daily lives.

I realize that I had the same opportunities to use my abilities that others have had. Some, however, were gifts with which I was born.

I understand that my first responsibility is the spiritual care of the congregation. I never stop thanking God for the opportunity to teach at a university.

When I want to forget the stress that is part of life, I count my graces and remember the ten years when I taught part-time at St. Benedict College. It was a joy that brought the mental balance that kept my sanity while at the parish in Hopeland. Some Americans had little sympathy for a priest who had come from Eastern Europe. No matter how hard I tried, I was constantly reminded that I was an immigrant. Yet, at the same time, the students and sisters from this pleasant college welcomed me cordially.

At the college, I created a second home while I was an assistant in Hopeland. For over ten years I was associated with a younger generation. I taught not only language, but Russian literature as well. I was very thankful for that opportunity.

May God be blessed and glorified that, in His kindness and mercy, a frightened priest who was not welcomed into this country should have equal opportunity to better himself.

As time passed, I reflected on graduate study while I was living in Canada. Through my new friends I matured more in my knowledge and in the pastoral ministry. Never did I imagine leaving the priesthood after finishing my study for my doctorate at the University of Ottawa.

Because of this, I felt better as a priest and as a human being. I did not allow myself to even think that I am or would be discriminated against. As a result, I realized I could not waste my time in this country. Becoming rich was not a high priority, but education was most important to me. In my heart, there is no conflict between theology and secular knowledge.

When I left St. Benedict College, I was informed by the administrators that, when I transferred to a larger university, I would be lost. Of course, I always have fond thoughts of the students and faculty of St. Benedict College who gave me a good start in my intellectual life. I also appreciated their prayers, hospitality, and their hearty acceptance.

I discovered that the large university in Richton, despite being crowded, was as pleasant a place as St. Benedict College. Who could imagine that the Polish priest from a small parish could make such great acquaintances with students, professors, and even the president of the university.

It would be impossible for me to forget the wonderful dean of the Evening College and Summer School who was once an organist at a Polish parish in the western part of Ohio. He is one of those people who is kind to everyone—students, faculty, and many others. Every day, he attended mass and treated me warmly. That marvelous human being is my friend, Dr. Michael Bonatelli.

On one occasion when I had to say good-bye to my class, I found that not only were there tears in my eyes, but pain in my heart when I told them that I cared for them and I knew that I probably would not see any of them again.

I told them, "Please treat people in your life with the same kindness and compassion that I tried to treat you. May God keep you well in His providential care."

That night as I prepared for bed, I was tired, but kind of proud that somehow my collar influences my friends and my students.

My experience in lecturing at the University of Richton is rewarding, now approaching approximately seventeen years from when I started there. The students, most of them are nice. I have a good feeling to work for them. I realize that the Russian language that I teach is not easy for Americans, but with their background and good will, they achieve a lot in their subject.

A very pleasant time also was when I had more classes such as the culture and civilization of Russia going through history; literature and culture really made me feel good because the response of the students was great. Lecturing and studying was successful, as shown through their oral reports and term papers and, of course, the final exam. All of that proved that Americans are smart. If they want to, American students can be excellent students. Some of the them proved it; many of them are good. Some just tried hard, and only a few flunked out or gave up.

Besides lecturing on literature and culture, the other beautiful experience was teaching language, which I have done for the second year of the course for eight years now. Teaching composition and conversation makes me feel good because of the successful achievement of American students who started with little but achieved a lot in the Russian language through translations, conversation, and grammar exercises.

I just love to see a senior student in the classroom. I had a reverend minister who was over sixty years old, and another time there was a professor with Ph.D.'s and great experience in teaching. But in the last semester, there was someone who will never be forgotten by me or by the other students in our class.

One day a gentle voice on the telephone from the administration at the university asked me if I would accept a sixty-plus year old senior citizen student, and I said okay, under the condition that I could contact this person to see if she should start with me or with the first-year Russian classes. But, when Natasha introduced herself and told me that she was *seventy-five* years old, without reservation or further questions, I really felt like saying, "Honey, come to the classroom." However, I didn't say that, as you have to be very careful as to what you say. You could be sued for talking in a way you consider nice to someone you do not know.

I cordially invited her to come to the class under the condition that she study in the classroom and must also accept the quizzes and tests that are given to all the students and turn in homework and also work in the class. Not long ago, I told Natasha that she is one of the best senior students that I have had in my career of teaching. The whole class loved her.

I am alert that I am a priest. I love that and am very happy to have the privilege to wear my Roman collar in the classroom on the campus of the university. Honestly, I understand that I can't mix religion with teaching. But outside of teaching, somebody who knows me and is away from the campus, through telephone conversations or visiting me at the rectory at St. Agatha's, if they ask me for spiritual leadership or assistance for pastoral service, I will oblige. They are people connected with the university, but how could I say no?

So, among them there are students, even faculty and administrative staff, who approach me for my spiritual assistance.

There was Nicole, a secretary in one of the departments. Nicole Divolve, her name had been changed from Wolanowski, which was her father's name, called me to ask me for assistance to help her father to be reunited with and reconciled with God after his difficult, long life of over eighty years, but under one restriction or reservation.

She said, "Be prepared, Father Michael, as he may be tough and unkind towards you. Perhaps he may even chase you away from his hospital room."

I assured Nicole that I would be brave and take any nastiness from her father, as I had to do the best for God's glory as a priest and also for the satisfaction of his daughter. I asked her for her assistance in going with me. She did.

I went with fear, but also with hope of the help of our Lady of Czestochowa. I took her picture that she would help me to assist Bronislaw in his conversation after many years of being away from the Church and God.

When I approached him with the picture in my hand, not intending to show it to him, with his sick-looking eyes, he looked at the picture and then at me.

He said, "Father, that picture reminds me of my native city in Poland, Czestochowa."

I saw tears in his eyes, and with his smiling face, I knew it was a miracle that, from a tough man, this tiger changed into a polite, gentle lamb and that I, as pastor of the flock, was able to give the hand to the one in one hundred who was lost but was brought back to God. It was successful as he received the Sacrament and said *thanks*.

Nicole jumped, cried, and screamed with joy. I felt like doing the same thing, but it wouldn't be proper to act like that, since I am a priest of the Roman Catholic Church and should act with dignity.

This incident makes me feel great. I waited seventeen years for just this situation, for Nicole to call me to help her father to be united and reconciled with God, and in it I am successful. I love it. So, teaching and preaching do work together.

There is no doubt that my predecessor worked hard and was committed. People liked and respected him, and maybe loved him, and this was very difficult for me, the new pastor. It would have been good to allow a couple of years to observe what things needed to be done on the church property, as well as to get to know the congregation so that I could help them spiritually, but unfortunately, there was no time.

I experienced the adjustment to the new place in many ways. I do not regret that I went ahead with some projects on the advice of a friend and with great determination. I remodeled, fixed, and repaired the church buildings and property. It was not easy.

One of the ways of supporting our church is social activities. How can we survive in some parishes without the extraordinary assistance of our people, our parishioners and our friends, the good, Christian hard-working people who spend hours giving generously of their time to support the cause for keeping up the material needs of a parish? I do appreciate their efforts and commitment and feel very grateful to them, and I often attend such social activities.

I despised asking for donations, but somehow the projects were successful. There were many other things that needed to be repaired, and with the kind help and generosity of the good people, the problems and difficulties were overcome.

For many years we helped poor people with collections for food, and also, for many years in this country, we had collections for Poland. The people of St. Agatha's are also sensitive on so-called *second collections* for assistance for needy people and helping missionaries who work in places like Somalia and other needy countries. And, of course, from time to time somebody stops and asks for money for gasoline or sandwiches.

Finally, there is the tendency to introduce friendship into the pastoral ministry. There is honest love in friendship. I observed throughout my many years of the priesthood, whether as assistant, chaplin, or pastor, through the liturgy and administering of Sacraments and counseling and through teaching and ministering to the sick and dying, that the center of it all was the feeling of love for each other.

I have met many priests and felt great respect for them. I understood their need to be with their friends and families. I knew that it was good to be with people I love. Perhaps it was simply to be with people I loved, to see their smiling faces and to have the feeling of love radiating through them from our loving Father.

Good friends encourage a priest's spiritual life. I believe that God sends these people to His priests to help them administer, teach, and organize.

Sometimes people misunderstand the affection paid to a priest. There is no intention other than to share friendship. Occasionally, some people are unpleasant and leave the parish because of something petty and small. But God shows His kindness and goodness through friends, and for it, He should be blessed. For all those friends I pray that I will always be grateful that they surround me, cheer me, and help me to be a good Christian and priest.

From time to time I am seen in uniform by my parishioners and others, or lecturing at the university, where I am happy to do so. By these activities I show that I am extending my pastoral ministry to others. I am not selfish, and I work through Him that God may be praised for the Good News, His Gospel.

I have been fortunate that some of my students and parishioners have found my work helpful. One of my students wrote a letter that I would like to include here:

> I have had the privilege and opportunity to help proofread and organize some of the manuscript for this book. As I read through it, I thoroughly enjoyed it and was impressed by the fact that it was such an exact interpretation of who Father Michael is.
>
> I first knew him as an instructor at the University of Richton and then as a friend, too. Even though he experiences the troubles in everyday living with the plumbing or the prevailing trash or intruders, the love of God, the Church, and his friends always prevails. He deals with the reality of maintenance like everyone else, but his reflection of what is good is constant.
>
> While he loves to be involved at the university in his teaching and the military activities, which are both people-related, his focus, which is his life, is to portray the love of God to whomever he meets. The genuine love to help people is what Father Michael is all about. He doesn't try to convert anyone in the classroom, though we know he is a priest by his collar. We somehow receive from him the message of a loyal friendship with us and the demanding as a colonel, but in reality as soft and tenderhearted as his teddy bears.
>
> There is no doubt in my mind that, when others read about Father Michael, they, too, will find a new friend.

In addition to the letter, there is, in my collection of poems, one written by Angelina, president of the Parish Council of St. Agatha's. It was written a few years after I arrived from Poland and after I became the pastor. It is sincere and simple, but in a beautiful way Angelina shows her appreciation for the pastor and, perhaps, tries to cheer me up.

> Sixteen short years ago, there came to this land
> > penniless, friendless and met with no welcome of a band;
> A foreign-born wanderer, but not for long,
> Who struggled and survived to belong.
> Who in this land of opportunity of ours,
> Added much beauty with love and flowers,
> As pastor of St. Agatha's parish—
> Pastoral care of which we will long cherish.

In the poem she says that she really truly meant what she wrote. It was a tribute to someone who through his commitment did change St. Agatha's spiritual and material conditions for the better.

The observations that I have included here were put down on the advice of the publisher of my first book, *The Priest Who Came to America*. I have tried to share these experiences in the ministry to try to help Americans appreciate who they are and what they have. Today the philosophies of life are difficult and the attitudes toward the Church and state are different. It is not easy living now and, at the time, being a mediator between God and the people of God.

To be successful in this matter, one needs someone who is in this position. God is the one who calls a man to the vocation of proclaiming His Good News. But, man is human and has his weaknesses; he is enthusiastic in his desire to serve and, yet, is often unable to fulfill this obligation because he becomes discouraged.

A priest, like all men, depends upon others to support him. I have discovered that there are many upon whom I must depend. Friends are those who understand, who do not condemn my weaknesses, but who encourage me with their prayers and advice.

I clearly recall one such friend and adviser, Father Mark O'Malley. We had many conversations, and one in particular was very helpful to me. It was just after I became pastor at St. Agatha's

Church. I arrived with twenty pounds of potatoes, a farewell gift from him. I asked my former pastor if I could keep my old apartment for a few weeks longer while I tried to get settled into my new ethnic parish, which is entirely different from a territorial parish. Father O'Malley kindly said that I might stay a while.

"Do you remember when I came to your parish," I asked, "and I told you that I was foreign and Polish?"

"Yes, and do you know what I said?" Father Mark asked.

"Yes, I do, and I treasure it in my heart. You welcomed me as a brother and as a part of the family of your parish," I replied.

I still remember that and still occasionally go to visit and to have lunch with some of these old friends. I feel that I left a part of myself in that parish. Those people were supportive and pleasant.

Once, I was invited to have dinner with Father Mark, and he noticed that I was depressed and asked me how I was feeling.

"I guess I tried the best, but do you know how I feel?" I asked. "I took over a Polish parish, people of my background. They advised me to collect money for a one-way ticket back to Poland. Why should I not feel depressed? I cannot seem to get these people to welcome me to the parish."

Father Mark responded, "Remember this; when you return to your parish and meet some of the people who give you a hard time, keep your head high. You are not at fault here. Your friend, the mayor of this city, Stanley Barron, also told me to tell you not to let them destroy you. Our mayor understands the position you are in."

I thanked Father Mark and promised to do everything I could to commit myself to my new assignment.

"Also, please remember, you are always welcome to come back home."

Later, Father Mark retired. He soon became sick and finally had to go live in a rest home, but before that I autographed one of my books for him. I can still remember that sad look from my friend when I last saw him. I thank God for calling such a man to the priesthood.

I also began to realize that self-confidence is the most important thing after God and friends. I realize that I can do anything with the help of those who love me. It is important to follow the rules in spite of how difficult it may be. A priest's life and liturgical rules, problems of administration, and upkeep of the property in a parish takes a great deal of energy.

Besides having priestly duties, as a man I must be able to do those things which make me a whole person. Those include my teaching and my duties as a chaplain. I am so very thankful that I can have all of these in my life.

I soon had an opportunity to visit Father Thomas O'Brien, an eighty year old priest who is now chaplain in a Catholic rest home. He is still healthy and strong, and I enjoy his sense of humor. I stopped by shortly after I received the pictures of me in my military uniform. I wanted him to see them.

"Father Michael, is that really you? Why don't you put a picture of you as a priest and one of these side by side in your study? You have so much for which to thank God that he allowed you to do good things in your life. You realized much more than you probably ever imagined," he said.

On the way back home, I reflected upon what Father Mark and Father O'Brien had said to me. Without God's guidance and blessing, that little boy in Poland would never have become a priest in the Roman Catholic Church.

I hope that the readers will pray diligently for the vocation of the priesthood and other religious vocations and that they will support those who come to serve them.

Finally, two very special anniversaries have arrived. I celebrated forty years in the priesthood and twenty years as the pastor at St. Agatha's Church. I want to let the readers know how grateful I am to God, friends, and parishioners for such an achievement. I also want to explain how I celebrated the occasion of my Jubilee.

These two anniversaries together had the character of spiritual renewal. I would like to mention what I said in my sermon on this Jubilee celebration.

"My dear parishioners, I cannot believe how time passes by so fast; it was twenty years ago Wednesday when I became pastor here at St. Agatha's.

"Like any beginning, it is difficult, and so it was no exception for me. As I have mentioned to you several times, being your pastor,

I learned a beautiful American slogan from my friends, 'Count the graces.' So, going through my years of being with you and being in the priesthood, yes, I see many graces, a lot of joy and happy moments, perhaps achievement and success.

"In spite of everything, the Church of St. Agatha did not collapse. We do give spiritual guidance and service. We did and we do this service for parishioners, and sometimes for their relatives, and our friends connected with St. Agatha's parish family.

"If I mention that I am happy to be the pastor at St. Agatha's, and somehow successful, the credit goes first to God and to my Church superiors, close friends, parish staff, students of the University of Richton, and cadets of the United States Army where I am chaplain at the Voluntary Battalion of Ohio at the University of Richton. But above all, I was *sent* to you, dear parishioners. If you wonder why I've stayed with you for so many years, I respond very honestly that it is because you are good people, good Americans and good religious Christians. My commitment to God and to you is paid back by the good condition of the parish; we do not owe anyone anything. The buildings are in good shape, and spiritually we don't feel bad because we did not miss any occasion to administer the Sacraments, and also to be personally involved in instruction before baptism, children receiving First Communion, Confirmation, and for blessing of marriages and other occasions.

"It happened so beautifully because you supported me, assisted me, and especially, I am grateful for almost twenty years to the presidents and representatives of the parish council who all worked with me and were very good assets and blessings for the parish. They did very well not only to cheer me up, but encouraged me to do the best for our common good for God's glory and, of course, for our salvation.

"I have to stress this: I never was hungry being with you, and was not worried about what I would have to wear and was able to pay not only for books and eyeglasses, but even for my car. Again, thanks to you and Divine Providence for providing very well in my life for these past twenty years and as I saw for many years how Divine Providence provided for you in your lives. It is true that I did not see anyone in the parish living in poverty or being abandoned, although we can't help seeing people suffering because of sickness. I am very happy to serve and pray for them at St. Agatha's and to give them encouragement and Sacraments.

"There could be a lot of talk about these past twenty years here, but first let me finish my personal feelings and sincere statement. It was worth it to be ordained and to spend one-half of my priesthood in Richton, Ohio, at St. Agatha's Church. I love it and praise God today for giving me the opportunity to be His and your priest/servant. For your kindness, accept my best wishes that you live a happy, successful and healthy life.

"Please don't wonder about tomorrow; just remember what Jesus said, 'Tomorrow will take care of itself.' So, today is a time of thanksgiving and a time of praising God for graces granted for twenty years being with you and forty years of my ordination. I say thanks to God for my strength, and thanks to you people of St. Agatha's for your kindness and support.

"Finally, please promise today that you will pray for vocations to the priesthood. Do believe me, I love to be what I am in spite of difficult times sometimes. I want to say to young Americans to be priests in the future; please take care of proclaiming the Gospel to the present and for the next generation. Amen."

Who would have imagined twenty years ago that I would stay for a long time at St. Agatha's? I know that many friends told me that I would stay here no longer than three years. But, thanks to God, I have enjoyed and endured these years that have gone by so quickly. I am glad to be here.

All of it has given me strength, and somehow I have been able and perhaps even talented not only in making up my sermons, but also fixing healthy and delicious meals for myself.

But, above all, I have experienced a more peaceful life being by myself at the rectory, especially since I was brought up in an orphanage where thirty-five to seventy-five boys were in one room. Of course, through my time in the army and through the seminary, I remember that there were some characters that I had to watch out for in order not to be hurt by them. My feeling of family life and having relatives wasn't the same as so many other people who were fortunate to have parents and siblings. But, I say that God saved me from some terrible kind of family, with fighting, harassment, and arguing, such as I have observed in the lives of some people that I have worked with.

6

God Shows Us Through Other People That We Are Not Forgotten

It is true that God shows His presence, kindness and compassion through those people who surround us. In this chapter Father Michael discusses the beautiful personalities, such as the bishops, priests, parish council members, friends, and those military people who are very dear to him.

The author realizes the greatness and kindness of our Lord who has come into his life through the people he has known. This is obvious because he has not been forgotten, but promoted with recognition, as well as kindness and friendship.

Teaching at the university has helped me to keep a mental balance, and serving as an army chaplain reminds me of my youth and my involvement against enemies, not only of Poland, but also much of Eastern Europe. I also realize that my youth was taken away because of the horrors of war.

In May of 1995 was the fiftieth anniversary when World War II was won by the Allies over Hitler's armed forces, the Nazis. It is amazing that fifty years have passed by me, too, but I have accomplished a lot in my life. As I often say, "Thanks to God and to my friends who are generous and religious." Among them have been nuns, priests, workmen, colleagues, and some from the seminary and colleges. I appreciate them, pray for them and have a great deal of love for them. But, in that group are also soldiers, officers, generals, and comrades. So, even if I changed the rifle for a chalice, the military life to church pastoral ministry, I still love and respect military people, pray for them, and I am happy to be a part of them in the United States Army. I am happy to be have been commissioned a colonel–06 in the Ohio Military Reserve. This was a peak moment in my life after my ordination.

After all the emotions that someone could go through on the occasion of forty years in the priesthood and twenty years at St. Agatha's parish, I sat down again under the gazebo and recalled what happened over six months ago when I was commissioned in the Ohio Military Reserves with the rank of colonel–06.

It was a great feeling and a happy experience when the United States rewarded me with the rank of colonel in the Army of the United States of America and I was sworn into the Ohio Military Reserves. Then, I started to realize how important to me, besides my pope, my bishop, and my brother priests, are also the officers of the army where I serve; among them are high-ranking generals whom I would like to mention.

I know they were and are very good models for all of us in the service. It doesn't matter if one is an officer or commander of some outfit, chaplain, or some other in the service of the United States Army. To become a general with the approval of Congress is a great tribute from the country, as well as a great privilege for those who commit themselves to the service for the soldiers and the leadership of those in the the armed services.

It is a good feeling to wear the uniform of the United States Army chaplain with the rank of colonel–06.

When I was asked to participate for the first time at the Ohio Military Reserve staff meeting, I felt great elation. I was welcomed by the commander general, a group of generals, colonels, majors, and other ranking officers of this unit. We have a staff meeting, or briefing, in a nice, clean hall at one of the restaurants on the road from Richton to Hopeland.

I was introduced to the group of officers by Commander General Bob and was pleased that we started with prayers which I conducted. It was a prayer of invocation, thanking God for the opportunity to gather together with high-ranking officers from the post of the commander of the headquarters of the Ohio Military Reserve.

In my remarks to the officers, I mentioned Normandy D-Day and the heroes of the battlefields, to whom I said thank you in my name and the millions of people who survived and also for those who died, fathers and grandfathers of the present generation of Americans who made the supreme sacrifice. 450,000 of them died for our freedom by crushing the powerful Nazi Armed Forces. For six years, this powerful force occupied, executed and terrified millions and millions of European people, but your forces were stronger and we were able to free those people from the oppressor's hand. My thoughts are of them, also of the the fifty year anniversary of the end of World War II and the victory over the Nazis.

The meeting was cordial and brotherly, so I committed myself to the comrades of mine at the headquarters of the Ohio Military Reserve that, anytime when they wished to talk with or pray with the chaplain, I would be there. I gave them my telephone number and said that I was open-minded to my officers, family members and soldiers if they needed or wanted to talk to me. It would be my great privilege to serve them as chaplain.

As a chaplain, I not only serve the Reserve Officers Training Center at the University of Richton, but am often asked to participate in celebrations of the Air Force and Army R.O.T.C. I am very happy to do so.

While getting ready for the President's Award at both the Army and Air Force R.O.T.C. at the university, I got a telephone call from my friend Mark's father, Eugene Smiley, to make a surprise visit at the Air Force museum which was in the process of being organized. *Oh, my gosh, I was asked to be in my colonel's army uniform.*

Well, when the time came, I put on my army uniform and went with Mr. Smiley to the museum. Upon entering the hangar where a few planes were located, my eyes glanced on one particular plane. I recognized the Polish insignia on the plane, so I approached it.

Mr. Smiley said, "We need you to translate the Polish and Russian signs in the plane."

He told me that this was a Russian MIG, which was a quick combat air force plane and was very successful in action, but it was probably built in Poland for the Polish Air Force activities when Poland was a Russian satellite country.

I was astonished. I was moved and emotionally touched by seeing something in Richton from Poland besides me, a colonel. I wanted to hug it; I wanted to kiss it, but it was too big and too dirty to even be touched. It was in the process of being restored to its original condition for flying once again.

When I questioned how the plane was brought to this country, no clear explanation was given, but I promised to write a poem in the future, entitled "Military Meeting of Colonel Michael With a Polish Plane," even if it was a Russian model but made in Poland for the purpose to protect and defend. Still, how this plane landed in Richton is a mystery to me.

Besides this one plane, I saw altogether about nine planes being prepared for an airshow at the beginning of September for the local public with the intention of having a permanent museum of planes which were used in World War II and others.

After this visit, I had dinner with Eugene Smiley and a friend of his. Then, when I went back home, I couldn't sleep; I kept thinking about how nice it was that older gentlemen, who specialized in different aspects of restoring planes, were working on the planes with so many parts. It really encouraged and cheered me to see these elderly men working away. I got the message that the legacy of the military comrades will be passed beautifully to the future, and I was also told that this was all voluntary work.

"Oh, yes," I said. "Eugene, the gentlemen should be commended and applauded for the noble activities for this wonderful country."

The uniform of the military always had special significance for me. When I am surrounded by officers and cadets, I am very happy. They represent self-discipline, politeness and brotherly respect toward me and to each other. I am reminded of the time when I was on the battlefield.

It is true that soldiers who face death on a daily basis care about each other. They went to death together, in each other's arms, giving up their lives, making the greatest sacrifice for freedom and the ideals that are so important, ideals for which soldiers pay so dearly.

There are many occasions when I have an opportunity to wear my uniform. Besides being their chaplain, I feel a special friendship being with them in uniform.

The last Christmas party was organized by Major Larry and his family. It was held in their beautiful house which had been especially prepared for the officer and his family. This meeting was an example of the closeness which those in the military feel among themselves. As chaplain, I had the opportunity to offer my thoughts and prayers in the best Slavic tradition, wishing them a long, happy life.

On the following day there was commissioning for the R.O.T.C. cadets of the University of Richton. There were not too many of them because it was in the middle of the academic year. Army regulations were adhered to. I was able to open the ceremonies and to offer a prayer. Afterward, I offered my remarks and a benediction. I mentioned D-Day, which happened fifty years ago, and was a victory which should not be forgotten.

I remember when I was in the Polish Army as a combat soldier, a corporal. But, I was mature enough to understand how important this victory over the Nazis was to all Europe. I also understood the importance of the Allied participation in freeing the millions who were victimized. I am thankful for the millions who survived, for the many millions of men and women who served.

I sat with other officers and representatives from the university. The cadets were smiling because they had become lieutenants in the U.S. Army. After the benediction, I told Major Larry that the event had been well organized and that he was a good officer and commander.

A day after the commissioning, I was privileged to meet with the commander of the Ohio Military Reserve. As I went to the meeting, I was hopeful that I would be established as a permanent chaplain, not only for the R.O.T.C. at the university, but as a permanent American military chaplain in the Reserve. Now, it would be a privilege to wear the uniform as an official chaplain in the Ohio Military Reserve.

The interview was cordial, and the general was very receptive. I was told that I had impeccable credentials for the position. The paperwork was delivered to headquarters, and then I went back home to get ready for Christmas in my parish. I said five masses that weekend and greeted my parishioners on Christmas. The gifts and Christmas cards I received, from the teddy bears to the practical gifts, made me happy.

The second visit to another general had been planned eleven months before. Larry and I had been invited by the chairman of the Joint Chiefs of Staff, John Shalikashvili. There were many reasons why I cherished the opportunity to meet with him. We both are natives of Warsaw, Poland, are in the service of our adopted country, and rose through the ranks to our present positions in the army. On the day after Christmas, after much preparation, Major Larry and I left Hopeland to visit the general. Both of us carried our uniforms. I took my Polish uniform to meet with the general, and I also carried letters from General Bob telling General Shalikashvili that he fully supported me in my appointment to the Military Reserves.

The night before the meeting with General Shalikashvili, Larry and I met with a representative of the Polish embassy who said that we could rest at his place. Jerry, who lived close by with his family, shared food from their Christmas Eve meal and a tradition for generations, Polish vodka.

In the morning we headed toward the Pentagon. We knew what entrance we were to use and that the representatives of the general and the chaplain's office would be waiting for us close to the time of our appointment. Larry and I ate breakfast at the restaurant in the Pentagon and watched officers come and go from the building.

When it was time for our appointment, we were welcomed and escorted by members of the general's staff. When his door opened, my heart beat faster. With tears in my eyes, I shook hands with General Shalikashvili, who welcomed us cordially and invited me to sit down and have coffee.

I answered the general's questions about my military experience and chaplaincy at the R.O.T.C., as well as how I adjusted to my new home in the United States. The conversation was ended with a photo session of the three of us. I brought the general a poem, which I handed to him with a book of poems I had signed. We parted with warm handshakes. I will never forget my visit.

As we left, we were told that a special golf cart was at our disposal for a tour of the Pentagon. Our guide explained the historical significance of the picture hanging on the walls and other points of interest.

I thought, as I was touring the Pentagon, how fortunate I was and how fortunate everyone is that young men and women of the military were willing to sacrifice their lives for their country. I remember their role in establishing peace and freedom in the world and in defending those who had been occupied and deprived of their lives and freedom.

After our tour, the three of us went to lunch and talked as friends. Since our plane was leaving in a couple of hours, we left for the airport.

The general gave me a sweater with the symbol of the Joint Chiefs of Staff, and he told me that, when people saw me in this sweater, everyone would be reminded to do their best. I also brought back a letter thanking General Bob Young for his help.

Before we left Washington, we visited Chief Chaplain John Robinson's officer, where we met with the deputy chief of chaplains. I saw the insignia of the men and women chaplains and the yarmulke on the Jewish chaplain colonel's head. The deputy chief was friendly and encouraged us to do our best in our commitment to the chaplaincy. He gave me a letter to a friend, who is a bishop, supporting my military commitment.

Larry and I fell asleep on the plane, as our trip had been tiring. When we landed, my cousin, Amy, met us and invited us for dinner, after which we both returned home.

The next day I went to see General Bob, who welcomed me to his office and addressed me by my new title. I knew something good had happened and that this was a very important day in my life. A copy of my appointment letter officially making me now assistant chaplain, Headquarters Reserve, rank of colonel–06, was given to me. With tears in my eyes, I thanked the general for the promotion. I was happy and realized that it was as important to me as my ordination or the reception of my Ph.D. I would be sworn into the Military Reserve in a brief ceremony at a later date.

On the way home, I prayed to thank God that I had not been forgotten, either by God or by people. My dream had come true.

As I sat at my desk writing, I received a phone call from one of my favorite officers. We had served at R.O.T.C., and he had called to wish me a happy New Year. I shared my news with him about being promoted to a colonel in the Reserve. We wished each other the best for the future. Friends do not forget each other, and when he stopped to visit his family, he called to acknowledge his friend.

Besides American colonels and generals, whom I have met and respected very highly, I have to admit that one four-star general in the Polish Army has earned my great admiration. He has had a most unusual journey from a prison in Siberia to this promised land. As a young lieutenant in the Polish Army during World War II under General Anders and later promoted through the battlefield, he became a leader of several outfits. He spent time in Iraq, Iran, and in other countries, and after he came to this country with his wife and two daughters in the late 1950s, General Tadeusz Dobry became the representative to the Polish Republic government-in-exile for the United States. He did an excellent job, as he did with all his assignments.

When Poland observed the fiftieth anniversary of the German invasion and occupation in 1989, following the orders of the president of the Polish Republic-in-exile, General Dobry contacted many veterans to promote them to higher rank and to decorate them with distinguished Polish medals, crosses, and decorations which they deserved. This included hundred of Polish veterans who fought with the British forces or in the Polish underground in Poland. I, too, having been in the Country Army and First Polish Army on the front line, was decorated and promoted to a colonel.

A couple of weeks ago, I was given a most wonderful opportunity to meet this gentle, noble hero and friend of our veterans, Tadeusz Dobry. I flew from Ohio to Chicago where he resides. This meeting was very emotional and dear for me and for the general. I felt it when I shook hands and hugged him and his family and during our conversations. Several times while I was with him and his family, I saw tears in his eyes. My reaction was the same.

The old general and his family treated me as a member of the family during the two evenings and one day that I spent with them. For good-byes, we promised to stay friends for the rest of our lives. Of course I was in my United States chaplain's uniform. I saluted him and was happy to have met a great hero, a great soldier, a remarkable general.

I will not forget the general for the rest of my life. I promised to pray for him. He shared with me his experiences, his achievements and his suffering, and I will treasure these in my heart and my memory forever. It was one of the most wonderful meetings in my life with the general who was going through hell in Siberia, but God helped him to come to this beautiful country.

When I got back home, there were some things I had to do to get ready for the commissioning. I had to go to buy a uniform at the military base.

I didn't realize that some military bases are located far from civilization. The base where I went was not far from Pittsburgh, and the people there were very pleasant. I was surprised that there are so many hills there and wondered how people drove in the snow and on ice in the wintertime. It was more casual than really big cities like New York and Hopeland.

The purpose of my trip was to buy more uniforms, and I was proud and happy when I saw my colonel's insignia and when I used my newly issued military ID to buy them at the PX.

After many hours on the road, I returned home. As soon as I returned, I called my commander to locate a good tailor to make the necessary alterations and also to sew on my insignia.

While I was at the tailor's, the woman who measured my pants reminded me of how older people still had to work. There were two women at this place, and they told me that they had a contract with the R.O.T.C. at the university to alter and to sew insignia on uniforms.

It was a cold Saturday when I was to pick up my new uniform, and I could hardly wait. But first I had to shovel snow from the walks in front of the church. While I was shoveling and before I was sworn into the Army Reserves as a chaplain, I wondered if there was anyone who would help me. Not often did I ask for help from my parishioners, and I felt that, working for the church, I was in a way repaying God for the many blessings He had bestowed upon me.

Furthermore, as I continued my reflections, my mind turned to my service to the soldiers, cadets and officers. I must say that I get a great deal of joy as I serve the U.S. Army as chaplain in commissionings; officers' promotions; military exercises, which I love; dining-in and dining-out; and the friendly lunches at my place in the parish house where there is a beautiful chapel, as well as where a Christmas party was organized by the commander.

Finally, my friend, Sister Michael Francis, who is a retired chairman of the English Department of one of the distinguished colleges of Ohio, once said, "Since you like the military uniform and look so dignified in it, tell us stories of how it happened that you became a military chaplain and how the uniform came to be one of the goals in your life."

It took a little time for me to respond to Sister Francis, about three years of meditation and reflection.

First of all, I was very happy when several years ago I was asked by one of my commanders of R.O.T.C. at the University of Richton to be a chaplain. Since I feel good towards the military people, I accepted the offer proudly and, of course, fulfilled my commitment with pleasure, dignity, and always with the intention to pay back those who were sons and daughters of this country who had died in Europe.

When I was a teenage soldier in the Polish Army, I heard enough stories of how good and great the American soldiers were. But, I never expected or imagined that the Americans would honor me so. So now everyone knows how it is that I became a grade colonel–06 in the Ohio Military Reserve.

The day of the celebration of my promotion was pleasant, and I took the oath to the military position of deputy chaplain with dignity. I, in the presence of the officers of the army and of friends, could not cry because it is not nice to be an officer in an army uniform and cry. But, in my heart, in my mind, and in my soul, I was thankful, joyous, and proud that I now was allowed to wear the uniform of the United States Army with insignias, crosses and silver eagle of a colonel.

Perhaps the president of the parish council of St. Agatha's described this situation best when she spoke at the celebration in the name of the parish, herself, and also in the name of the diocese of Hopeland.

"General Bob, ladies and gentlemen, officers of the United States Army, friends of ours, and Colonel Michael, it gives me great pleasure to welcome you, in my name as president of the parish council, members of the parish council, our dear parishioners, and the diocese of Hopeland, to this beautiful ceremony at St. Agatha's and for the opportunity to meet together here today.

"In recognition of this day, my remarks will be brief, as I don't want to cut the rest of the program short.

"It is always a pleasure to announce good news, and the occasion of today's event is good news for our parish that our pastor, the spiritual leader, is involved and *extends* his pastoral ministry to the United States Army and especially as he has done for the R.O.T.C. at the University of Richton for years.

"Today, I feel in my heart that, what happens today when Father Michael is sworn into the Ohio Military Reserve by authority of our government and by Major General Bob, commander of the Ohio Military Reserve, he deserves it and has earned it.

"Our parishioners and friends know that, behind the uniform or chaplain colonel, Father Michael has a good Polish-American heart and that he deserves to be in the service of the American

Army, in the Reserves, and to be in an American Army uniform as an American Army chaplain.

"Such an event as this one today should unite us more for us to try to do the best in our commitment for God and for our country, especially when an occasion like today shows you that, yes, it is worth it to work hard and that God does not forget people when they care about others, but rewards them during their lifetime.

"Thanks to all of you that you came on this kind of occasion to celebrate Father Michael's distinguished event. But I would also like to say that our parish is proud of having a pastor who is not only our spiritual leader, professor at the University of Richton, and chaplain, but also a darn good janitor.

"God bless you for making this day a reality for Father Michael and for the parish. Father Michael's dreams are now fulfilled.

"Congratulations, Father, Colonel Michael."

This was presented by Angelina, president of the parish council at the swearing-in on January 17, 1995.

As the writing of this book comes to a close, I want everyone to know that at heart I am a priest, then a teacher, and then a military person.

After the swearing-in ceremony, I waited for the mail. It wasn't long before Johnny, the mailman, stopped by to deliver the mail, which consisted of a bunch of letters, magazines, and junk mail. I question how anyone could buy so many things that people offer for sale through these publications. Among the group of offerings, one finds advertisements for bibles, perfumes, and cars. Ignoring all the propaganda I received, I picked out what came from the diocesan office as private letters to me and checked them out at once.

In between times of writing poems and novels, I ponder on what I should write that would satisfy the readers, and I think that I should point out what is going on in the beautiful Catholic Church which I have tried to serve so faithfully for the past forty years. My good friend, Sister Michael Francis, advised me to write something about the changes in the Church and how I feel about them.

There is no doubt that I, like many other hard-working priests, am concerned and have observed these changes. I think that I do adjust to it as easily as one can. Christ is always the center of my life. My experiences have shown the presence of Christ in the Church, as well. But from time to time, because I am open-minded, I have learned to like different people of different nationalities, different religions, and perhaps even to be happy about the good treatment of priests by the bishop, who has a kind of brotherly approach, encouraging them and helping them to do their best in serving God.

But, I am very disturbed when I hear some people complaining that there is no ordination of women into the priesthood. Many of them participate in groups of Catholics or other liberal organizations, which shows that they are frustrated, upset, mean, or depressed. So, I question how they could share the priesthood of Christ, which requires compassion, sacrifices, keeping our mouths closed when we are hurt by somebody, and counting the graces in our lives instead of complaining. This movement does not seem to work, especially since so many thousands of nuns have left the commitment in the religious life. I remember how nice and hard-working they were thirty years ago. Since early in my priesthood, they have rapidly changed their minds.

What has upset them? Many nuns have left the convents in the United States. If they did not like their comfortable lives in the community, praying and living together, how could some of them who want to be ordained live by themselves at a rectory and, at the same time, not only have to preach and administer a parish, but also to be a janitor? I know what parish life is because I care for a parish, teach at a university, give services to the army as chaplain, as well as write poems and novels. Besides all of these duties, in a small parish the priest must do the yard work, clean and cook, and pick up the trash and garbage that others leave in the church lawn. I do not complain, but accept it as reality.

With the strength and faith in the Archpriest Jesus and with love toward the Church and the people of God, I do not worry about the human approach to the changes in the Church. I know that the Holy Spirit will protect and defend it. It is wonderful to involve lay people in the pastoral ministry and perhaps to help in the administration of the parish, but the question is how, for many ages, were priests able to take care of the parish needs by themselves so well? The morals of the people were higher, respect for the Commandments of God was better, and the churches were not only beautifully and artistically built, but were filled with crowds of people.

I remember at the beginning of my priesthood listening to confessions for many, many hours. What has happened? Don't people want forgiveness for their sins? I encourage other priests and myself not to lose good priestly spirit and to do the best in their commitment to the mission of proclaiming Jesus' Gospel.

Also, from time to time I am disturbed about a too business-like tendency to organize parishes and to have a lot of bureaucracy from the central office for pastoral ministry. Above all, I know that to demand money from the people, to assign and to request, does not work. We may ask, we may beg, we may not receive, but at the same time I know that Divine Providence proves that He cares about us that we are not hungry and not behind in paying our bills and that we are happy to be what we are, ordained for God's mission and the salvation of us all.

Our faith comes to us through the teaching of the Holy Catholic Church. As a part of it, I realize that she's doing beautifully, from the time after the Resurrection of our Lord and His presence with the apostles for forty days when He established the Church and made the apostles the first bishops, to today, when we have the successor of St. Peter in John Paul II. The bishops in our diocese and in the whole world of the Catholic Church are intelligent, gifted, and devoted leaders of the flock in their commitment with their teaching.

We, as priests, try the best to commit ourselves also for proclaiming the Gospel and to serve our Lord, as well as the people of God, the best that we can according to our abilities.

Concerning the teaching and military service, I know that we are subordinated sometimes to many other superiors other than bishops. Yes, I could very honestly say that all the generals, commanders, staff officers of the R.O.T.C., as well as top officers of the Ohio Military Reserve, are beautiful people with intelligent leadership, great experience and great wisdom, that serve for this beautiful nation like the bishops who serve for the Church. Without bishops, there would not be a Church, and without good generals, there wouldn't be a superpower such as our country, ready to protect and to defend not only our nation, but others when there will be a need.

I do realize how great also are presidents, deans and chairmen of departments at the university not only in our city, but also in many other cities in the United States. They are not only protectors and promoters of knowledge of science, but also great scholars and scientists. I observe their willingness and being ready to share their knowledge with the younger generation, their students, and they are doing so well.

Finally, thanks to bishops, thanks to generals and thanks to spiritual leadership, we are surviving, and the Good News of the Gospel is proclaimed. And, under their leadership, we are ready to meet the twenty-first century.

Many powerful institutions have collapsed, but we survive and are ready to meet the twenty-first century with the beautiful mission of ours as priests, which is to proclaim the Gospel. It wasn't and isn't an easy mission. From time to time in the future, the Church will suffer, but I do believe strongly in Divine Providence and the power of the Holy Spirit and that the Church in the following centuries will flourish, will be successful, and all human beings will benefit from it.

After that reflection, I knelt down and prayed that God would help His Church to flourish and would bring religious people into the priesthood and other religious vocations.

Epilogue

One evening, shortly after the celebration of my Jubilee, I, happy and content, sat under the gazebo in the backyard of the rectory. My eyes gazed about in wonder at the flower garden nearby which is my pride and joy, since I spend much of my spare time there, weeding and cutting. The statue of our Lady stands among the flowers which bloom so beautifully, and the shrubs are nearby.

I recall some disasters like the one that happened not long ago in Japan, where so many thousands were killed and many became homeless because of an earthquake. Such occurrences are telling us something.

First of all, we are fortunate that such a tragedy didn't touch us, but we know from the media the strength and power of nature. It is able to destroy people and buildings which have stood for many decades. But, it also brings our attention to the realization that material things cannot be valued over spiritual ones. We build and we protect, but there is something else and somebody else who knows how to destroy it.

The lesson we must learn from it is very simple and directed to all human beings and that is that everything on this planet is temporary. Almighty God, through His Son, gave us instructions that our destiny is not of this earth, not temporary, but eternal.

In a reflective mood, I recall my first night at St. Agatha's parish. I compared it to this quiet, tranquil August evening. At that time, years ago, I was fearful and leery of the tasks that lay ahead of me, but I trusted that God would help me. On this peaceful evening, I can see the fruits of my labors. I have been working in God's vineyard, in this little place for twenty years, and a plentiful harvest lay before me.

I then rose to my feet and walked over to the church. Inside of the church, I knelt before the Tabernaculum and thanked God that the seed of His Word fell upon the good soil at St. Agatha's parish, where it had taken root, grown, and flourished.

In conclusion, I prayed in such a manner, "Heavenly Father, bless this beautiful country, which has adopted me, with peace, prosperity, and unity. Heavenly Father, please bless America."

I then went to the rectory to rest.

About the Author

Father Thaddeus M. Swirski, Ph.D., is the present pastor of St. Hedwig's Church in Akron, Ohio, where he has served in that capacity since 1974. From 1978 to the present, Father Swirski has also been an instructor of the Russian language and literature in the Modern Languages Department of the University of Akron.

Born in Warsaw, Poland, in 1930, Father Swirski participated in World War II from age 14 to 16, first as a partisan and then as a soldier of the Polish Army organized in the Soviet Union. During his service, he received crosses and medals for bravery in action.

After the war and more advanced education, he studied at the seminary and was ordained from the higher Seminary *Hosianum* of Warmia in Olsztyn, Poland, in 1954.

In 1962, Father Swirski immigrated to the United States and was permanently accepted into the Diocese of Cleveland in 1966, receiving that same year a Master's Degree in Russian Language and Literature from Case Western University in Cleveland, Ohio. And, after further graduate studies at the University of Ottawa, he received a Ph.D. in Slavic Studies in 1979.

At the time of the changing in Eastern Europe, Father Swirski was promoted to the rank of colonel chaplain in the Polish Army and was further decorated with several military medals and crosses for military service and for his work among his Polish-American parishioners. In December of 1994, he was appointed to the Ohio Military Reserve Army with the rank of colonel–06, and then commissioned on January 18, 1995. In addition to being deputy chaplain in the Ohio Military Reserve, he has served for ten years as chaplain of the Army R.O.T.C. Voluntary Battalion of Ohio.

Father Swirski started to write poems at the age of 14 and has continued to the present. His other published works include three collections of poetry—*The Beauty of Creation, A Touch of Divinity,* and *America, Quo Vadis?*—and this novel's prequel, *The Priest Who Came to America.*